Also by Charles Kerns:

Santo Gordo: A Killing in Oaxaca

Oaxaca Chocolate

A Santo Gordo Mystery

Charles Kerns

For pictures and more information about Santo Gordo:
http://facebook.com/SantoGordo
http://goo.gl/P9Ng7F

ISBN-13: 978-1492263845
ISBN-10: 1492263842

For the city of Oaxaca

With thanks to:
Professors de la Rosa and Zermeño for Spanish,
Michael Carter and Joe Patwell for English,
Señor Conrado for his neighborly knowledge of everything,
Dr. Carolyn Tsen for keeping me going,
Eduardo Pulido Zamora for his study of cabdrivers,
Mama and family for making me at home,
And Roshni for everything else.

CONTENTS

Posada

I needed coffee, but first I stopped at the big, pink, two-story *pastelería*. The sugar dough smell woke me a little. Not as good as coffee, but a start.

I walked in and took two big donuts—*donas* is what they call them down here—and got in line. Three girls in front dangling book bags dropped their money and giggled to each other, the same way schoolgirls do in the US. They took the bag of pastries from the clerk and giggled more going out the door.

Next in line, two guys, not local—maybe from Mexico City—muscled, big spiky hair, smoking. They stood in front of me but were talking to each other, ignoring the clerk, so I cut ahead. I was hungry. They gave me the look so I dropped some coins and headed out, leaving them and their dagger-arm tattoos dripping blood. I made a fast exit.

I was in a hurry and I needed some caffeine for dunking these babies, so I walked half a block over to my espresso joint, *La Avenida*, and got my seat, the heavy duty one, way in the back.

A while ago I snapped a chair leg when I sat down and they said, "Roberto, *nuestro amigo,* you are much too big for our chairs, but too good a customer to lose." A cook reinforced the chair with two steel rods and painted Santo Gordo in big blue letters on it. Everyone knew it was mine and to stay clear until I was finished for the morning. It was nice to be wanted even if they used that name that I tried to avoid.

You probably understand the Gordo part. I will tell you about the Santo later.

I was dunking away, turning my espresso into some kind of sweet mocha thing with the donut's chocolate melting in the cup when it happened.

My brain yelled earthquake when everything shook. The wall looked like it gave a little in the middle and the floor had a wave passing through the tile. I saw a flash too, but I didn't reason anything out. I just threw myself down. Then the boom blew out the front window and cut up the American sitting by it, the one who had arrived in Mexico that morning. He started yelling.

I crawled under the table with my eyes shut and bumped its legs and knocked everything over. The table would not do much good anyway if tons of rocks and cement came down in a quake, so having the thing lying sideways next to me was about as useful as having it over my head. I lay flat as my cup bounced a couple of times, splattering foam when it hit the floor.

My donuts survived–a minor miracle. They dropped on my chest and I grabbed them. Then I just held on, like it says to do in earthquakes, but there was no more shaking. Just the one boom and then after a minute someone outside yelled, "It's an explosion."

I looked over at the guy bleeding by the window while the barista wrapped a tablecloth around his arm trying to make a tourniquet out of the thing. It was turning red.

Some gringos were on their knees under tables. The Mexicans had run out of the building knowing you are dead when a concrete roof falls on you. One tourist couple in the back sat wondering what happened, still holding their coffees.

"A propane tank blew." Two Americans had gone out and kept us informed. "Some guy was pumping gas into the bakery from his delivery truck, the kind with the big twenty-foot propane tank."

I figured I would go take a look, but stayed near the wall, not like the Mexican crowd forming in the center of the street.

"Get out. If the truck goes, we're dead." One of the Americans had sized up the situation and did what anyone schooled with OSHA and US regulations would do. "It's going to blow," he yelled. My fellow safety-first Americans needed no more. They broke into a run, heading the other way.

I should have gone too but I stayed in the street with the locals. I had been in Mexico a long while and was picking

3

up good Oaxacan attitudes toward life and death and everything in between.

Flames spiraled out widows and cracks in the bakery. It was my pastelería, my bakery, the big pink building, where I had bought my donuts a few minutes before. I could have been as deep fried as my chocolate-covered babies, but something must have been watching out for me that morning.

I had been looking in on Mexican churches awhile and I hoped the Virgin, the one everyone prayed to, watched out for me like she did for the Mexicans. Later on, I would find out I was still on my own. She had not yet decided about me. She knew I still had gringo dreams about getting everyone to arrive on time and making the traffic flow better. Dreams I should leave up north.

The bakery was a mess. Stonework had fallen. Concrete beams cracked all the way from the roof two stories up, down to the street. Flames were on the roof too. The building was standing, but leaning a little. The explosion was not big enough to knock it down, but it was close and glass was everywhere.

In the middle of the street, in front of the broken building, the propane gas truck looked normal, except its right front tire was burning away. Flames and smoke twisted out the wheel well, like during one of the really bad protests when trucks and buses were torched and the crowd threw rocks and the police used sticks to hit everyone and chase the street clear. Luckily, Oaxaca had been at peace for a while, ever since the old governor left, so we tried to forget this sort of thing.

The driver had been pumping propane out of one of those big tank trucks. A hose wound from the back of the truck towards the bakery but ended abruptly in the street, chopped off, twisting and jumping like some crazed fire-snake. Flames shot out its frayed end. Cell phones were already pulled out to take pictures. "What a video," shouted a student from the local university standing with his friends in the street. "What a great hellish video."

It was hell. It looked like the devil spraying fire, like in the paintings that Catholics conjured up when they were really bad and had nightmares. I figured I would see this all again when my Mexican retirement ended and I could not make the grade for Saint Peter.

I was thinking, maybe I should move back a little, too. God and his Virgin can only protect the crowd and me so much. I knew that from my Protestant physics.

The man who drove the gas tank truck normally did nothing more dangerous than smoke a couple of cigarettes when he was pumping propane. But this time, he was holding on to the valve in back of the tank, shielded partly from the flames by a thousand kilos of pressurized gas ready to blow. He had wrapped his hands in rags to keep from burning them too much as he held the valve heated by the flames ten feet away. He turned it as quickly as he could. The loose hose slowed its wild jumping. The fire shooting out its end stopped. The valve was closed. The hose looked dead lying there after all that work dancing in the street.

It was different in the bakery. Flames had gotten bigger and heat was hitting my face even here half a block away.

Most firemen stood around in their long yellow coats and fire hats. I kept thinking that the government would want a picture in the newspapers the next day to reassure everyone, probably a big one in color.

One fire truck was pumping water. Even more firemen came and pulled the hoses from the side of another fire truck. They drenched the propane truck. In thirty seconds its tire stopped burning. Sooty smoke came out making a nasty black fog, low on the street, smelling like an old tire skid.

With this success, the firemen turned to the bakery. It was burning fast.

Buildings down here are stone or cement, so fires usually go out pretty quickly—no walls or roof to feed the fire, not like back in the States where we trust wood way too much. The bakery was not just cement, though. It had tables and counters and but worst was the oil for frying the donuts, and I was not even thinking about the propane gas tanks on the roof. This was a fight. Not simply a photo op for the firemen.

People in the street talked as they watched. Everyone had something to say, but they all understood that the gas truck was filling the propane tanks in the bakery when something went wrong. Maybe the hose was old. Maybe a connection failed. No one knew. Most would say God willed it. No one knew it was deliberate, a crime. They never would, but I would find out soon.

More fire trucks came.

I watched while they got everything under control. Smoke replaced flames. Firemen kept spraying the propane truck. The crowd moved towards it. Some even hid right behind the big tank so they would not feel the heat. This was Mexico and crowds did what they wanted.

People have freedom here that you never find in the States. Crowds block roads. They parade in the streets, sometimes in protest and sometimes just following around the Virgin Mary–called María here in Mexico. Police only watch. Most of the time.

Some younger men in the crowd walked right up with the firemen. God would watch out for them they figured. Not the police.

I stayed back a little and saw my bakery was done, well done. Oily water poured down by the curb and ended up in a pool covering the sidewalk where I was standing. Probably the same oil that fried my donut was leaking into my shoes.

The morning stayed confused. No traffic could get through. Police put yellow caution tape everywhere. No one walking paid much attention to it but cars sat and fumed when traffic cops stopped them. Buses figured out routes through other parts of the city. Most people walked. Car traffic was too slow to get anywhere. It was worse than the political blockades that happened every couple of days. This one had people coming to see what was going on, not simply trying to get around it.

I stayed in the cafe for a while. I couldn't think of a good reason to leave after things looked under control, so I ordered eggs, *huevos rancheros*, fried dead, as usual. I might stand next to a hot propane tank but took no chances with half-cooked eggs and their bacteria buddies.

One more espresso and I was pretty perked.

I listened in on the next table watching a YouTube clip showing the fire. A couple of versions were already up. On Twitter everyone was guessing how many dead people blew up.

The internet had invaded Mexico along with us gringos. Oaxaca used to be my cut-off outpost away from the States back when I got here six years ago. Phone connections were slow; mail was impossible. Now Oaxaca was in the middle of the world, just like everywhere else. And news went around the world fast. I was sure someone in China or Berlin or even Chattanooga or some such God-forsaken place was sitting down and watching my bakery burn right then.

Mexican disasters always have a long fatality list. Gruesome pictures make the newspapers the next day—bodies, car wrecks, and bullet holes are the main fare in what they call the *sección roja* in the newspapers. With the internet you could see them right away, no waiting for the morning. Disasters were globalized, like everything else. Even me—I went global when I retired. I never thought I would live outside of the States.

Everyone was saying it was a disaster miracle. *"¡Es un milagro!"* I heard it over and over. The owner of the bakery had run back and warned everyone. The customers got out and away from the windows, the windows where I saw my donut tray a couple of hours back. Even the workers upstairs made it to the street and no one died. Not like when the fireworks factory blew up last Christmas north of Mexico City.

There were burns, but nothing disfiguring. At least, where you could see them. That was the rumor. The gasman burned his hands shutting of the valve, but that was expected. Some people up to a block away were cut with glass, like the guy by the restaurant window. They had been taken away in new, fancy ambulances. Everyone lived. *"¡Es un milagro!"* Even I said it.

Some local women were already putting flowers and candles in front of the blown up bakery to make a street altar. The miracle of the Virgin of the Bakery, they said. She watched out for pastry chefs and us donut eaters too. I wanted to leave a tray of fat big ones, not candles, for her. She gets hungry too, I bet.

My eggs were long gone, but being retired left me a lot of time to sit and look. I did that in the mornings–I read the paper, watched people. But today the crowd, milling around, watching the bakery, got boring. Too many jammed the street. I could only see rear ends backed up to the frame where the window used to be. And then the cook brought out some plywood to cover it. It was time to head back to the apartment.

I left the cafe and pushed through the crowd. The fire was out and the street was full. A local TV crew holding cameras and microphones interviewed people in the street. They were pushing closer to the walls of the bakery. Police were standing around.

A Federal Police pickup went by and parked in the *Zócalo*, the main plaza in Oaxaca, across from the bakery. Cops dressed like soldiers stood in the back of the truck as usual, holding their rifles loosely, looking out through framework of metal pipes built over the pickup bed, a framework that looked made to carry two-by-fours or ladders or anything else, not the rifles and machine guns you could see, barrels poked out, not aimed anywhere in particular. Like usual. The soldiers just watched.

You never knew quite what was happening in Oaxaca. Anything could be political. Maybe the new governor was getting a donut when the bakery went off.

But I was pretty sure nothing like that happened that day. If it had, companies of soldiers along with their little helicopter, not just one pickup-truckfull, would be swarming along with God knows what else. The bakery was just one of those accidents, a broken hose, a big leak, a little spark. That was what I thought then. Something God did when he was bored, but then changed his mind and saved everyone, your basic Catholic miracle.

****

I started back to my apartment. I could walk in the street because no cars were moving. Everything was blocked after the explosion, except for one cab that found a place to turn around and was heading out of the mess, up on the sidewalk, down a one-way street, the wrong way. Some cars turned around to follow. Everyone else honked.

The cab pulled near me and I saw Efraím, my friend the *taxista* who had been with me when we dealt with the assassination last year, the assassination when I pulled a boy out of a bullet-filled car and later saved a village, at least according to some folks. That was when I got my Santo Gordo name. Really I was only trying to stay alive, but I became Santo Gordo in the newspapers and on some of the altars around here, especially the ones in my espresso stop and favorite restaurant. I let it go. I am not a saint, but it is easier to ignore stories and accept a few half-blessed *mezcals*, than to straighten everything out.

Efraím sat in his new taxi that he bought with the gold mine money. That was part of the Santo Gordo story too. His village, the one they say I saved, was sitting on a gold mine. His townspeople got a little. Not so much with the government and the officials and the political parties and the global companies scooping up almost everything. But they got a little, and part of that was enough for a taxi or two for Efraím. The village also got a mess from the diggings.

As usual with cars down here, his taxi shined like a factory newborn even though it was already nine months old. Cars age differently here. They know they are loved and fight harder against rust and time. Men cherish cars like lovers, and tart them up with chrome and leather, useless shiny parts that give them a style we gringos struggle to appreciate. And dirt, cars forget what it is, except for ones out in the countryside, on the farms full of mud and dust. City cars get a scrub every day and a shine on Sundays. They glow with new Mexican middle-class pride, the kind poor people have when they move up a little, the kind my father had when he got his 1950 Ford, his first car, and waxed it under a tree in front of the house every weekend with me doing the bumpers, back when I was a kid.

But it is more than that. Cars replaced old Zapotec and Mixtec Gods in these men's dreams. Cars, like gods, asked for sacrifice, money and time, but not blood–OK, a little when drivers sped and drank too much mezcal.

Cars replaced the horses of the conquistadors, too. Native peoples did not know where the armor-clad Spaniard ended and his horse began. The two were one, that man-beast that conquered Mexico. Now men are one with their cars, subduing villages with their traffic, noise and fumes.

Cars make men look good and give them style. Men must look good to compete in this new upscale world. Looking good is more important than being good. Everyone knows that.

"Hola, Efraím." I ran to catch the cab, but I don't go that fast anymore. He looked back, stopped and waved me in, laughing at my non-athletic efforts.

"No corras" Do not run. "I will wait. You get a great price for a taxi ride today–free." I understood his working Spanish. I could not talk Spanish philosophy yet, but I could yell for a cab. Efraím opened the front door for me.

He was a friend. One that moved to the top of my friend list when we got shot at together a while back, saving his village. He had been Americanized a little when he lived in the States, so my informal, not so stylish, gringo ways did not offend him too much.

I reached the cab. Efraím spared no expense on it. Purple florescent lights glowed around the *placas*–the license plates. The new little steering wheel made it hard to drive but was handmade, and the Virgin Mary glowed in the center over the horn button. I gave thanks to God for its front seats that swiveled out so I could get in without much bending. I am too big for most things in Mexico and appreciate something gringo-sized. But the seat was not bought for me. It was to show off to fellow taxistas. Most passengers sat cramped in the back.

Efraím looked in the rear mirror to see down the street where the bakery was still smoking and the fire trucks watching. "Your bakery is gone. We need an Americano mass–maybe last rites with some sacramental donuts for expats."

He gave me a hard time about my unbreakable gringo habits. Donuts were one of them. I gave him a hard time about anything I could think of, but that day I was stumped. I was just happy to get a ride home.

"Don't worry Señor Gordo." Efraím spoke in a consoling voice. "It will come back. The bakery made too much money from you Americanos who want to sit in the Zócalo and have a cheap snack. Places that earn like that one will never die, they will rise from the dead. Business resurrection is part of your US religion, is it not?"

That bakery was an institution down here. I figured he was right. The bakery would rise from the ashes.

I did not know exactly where Efraím was leading me. He had a way of guiding the conversation to a place that he wanted.

"I mourn the true Oaxacan restaurants, the ones that have only one or two loyal local customers a night. Their deaths are the hardest because they never rise from the dead. And they take the cook and the waiter with them if they cannot find another job."

I think the ones losing their jobs head up to Mexico City or the border. They do not die, but it seemed that way when they left and the city lost its people.

Oaxaca was struggling after the boom it went through when the city was the darling of those New York Times foodies. Writers discovered Oaxaca's *mole,* the sauce made with chilies and chocolate, and wrote articles about the cuisine. Earlier, everyone just called it *comida*–food. One writer even got the menu in Oaxaca listed as a UN world heritage. And probably stole the recipes for a cookbook.

Everyone came to visit back then. Tourists clogged the place and new restaurants opened, one a day, but after a year or two, a new fad started somewhere else, maybe in Morocco or Singapore or some such place and stole the fickle appetites of America's foodies. Oaxaca got checked off on tourists' lists. The gringos had eaten their hot chocolate meat sauce and chili-fried grasshoppers and drunk mezcal. Been there, ate that. Most did not come back for seconds. At best, they went to a Oaxacan restaurant in hometown New York or even Omaha or Kansas City where the immigrants who left Oaxaca worked. Foodies ran the place but got help from cheap Oaxacan cooks and dishwashers.

Worse for Oaxaca were drug gangs, not in Oaxaca, but up north leaving heads in the streets of Jalisco. Nasty murders scared tourists who did not see much difference among Mexican cities. No one knew that the drug wars

14

were way up in the north, not in Oaxaca. Down here, we just had normal violence. Nothing crazy–only an assassination here and there. And then, only of protesters or officials, not tourists. You should be scared down here, but scared of getting run over, not getting shot.

Efraím turned a corner and hit the traffic jam. Buses sat in blue, diesel smoke clouds. Cars were not innocent either. The fumes could pickle your lungs if you sucked enough in. Efraím inched his cab down the street. Walking would have been faster. But I was ready for company and wanted to talk about the explosion.

"They say no dead people in the explosion–a miracle. Lucky they did not see me getting a donut just before it blew up," I said, remembering the old Santo Gordo stories about me. I could have been held responsible for the miracle.

"I hate to tell you, Señor Roberto, my gordo friend, my saint friend, but they do have that picture. A reporter has it, and we know it will be out in the papers tomorrow. Then the police may want to know what you were carrying so carefully in the picture. You held on like it might blow up if you dropped the thing."

I could not tell if he was joking. Efraím knew everything going on in the city. He had the eyes and ears of all the cab drivers keeping him posted. His radio crackled with news about routes, reroutes and every once and a while, news about what the police were doing. I would not be surprised if he knew about someone taking my picture.

I started to explain, "I was carrying chocolate donuts, nothing exploding, just donuts."

"I know, but stay on your toes." He patted my shoulder like a big brother. I was the bigger, older guy, but Efraím was the one who knew his way around.

"Anyone else there at the bakery?" he asked casually, but stared right through me. Like a cop.

"I don't know." I stammered it out. "School girls and some young thug types. Big, gelled hair, like all young guys have. But tattoos too."

That was a little unusual down here. Tattoos were a more up-north thing. "I didn't pay attention. I was there for donuts."

"You still have the donut evidence in case the *policía* asks?"

I figured that was a joke. Everyone knew how long donuts lasted around me, but this was weird. Efraím seemed worried. He usually only worried about his cab, his family and his village. And his friends. You needed to prioritize down here.

"Roberto, some advice–don't talk about this. No one was there but you and the schoolgirls. Remember."

I was famous in the expat gang for two things, well lots of things, but two were relevant. I talked a lot and I ate a lot. Efraím had been coaching me into being a strong, silent Mexicano but I needed more work. Some days, especially after a mezcal or two, I had no shutoff, but I would remember his warning.

A call came in on the radio.

"I will be there in five minutes," Efraím always said that. Nothing was more than five minutes away no matter how long it took to get there.

16

"We are near your place and I need to pick up a fare. Let's talk later."

I got out and looked back as he drove off. Something was wrong.

****

My house was just a block away. But the government had decided to improve Oaxaca. And maybe their wallets with a little graft money. The construction slowed me down. Streets were going to be new, at least in the tourist areas, but appear old, with fake cobblestones and a sidewalk that looked carved out of rock. They had rubber molds, about twenty feet by ten feet, looking like inside-out rocks that they tamped down on wet cement. Then they aged it with a little color. Oaxaca was getting older looking. Except where everyday people lived. There it was just getting messier.

Wires were going underground for the tourists. Big plastic sewer pipes were going in. Flat sidewalks without foot-trapping holes, a concept long overdue, were coming so tourists could look around, daydream and maybe buy something as they wandered around, not paying any attention to their feet.

Who knew what the people who lived here would get besides the bill. Everyone involved in the construction, except for the workers, would do well though. Lots of money was going around. I guess it is the same everywhere–rich neighborhoods get it, poor ones need it.

In front of me, there was dirt, no pavement yet and a long ditch running down the center of the street, a neat one with straight deep sides, six feet down and three feet across. A blue plastic pipe lay at the bottom. It was the new sewer. Wires, tubes and more plastic pipes ran every which way through the hole, some buried deep but most about a foot below the surface. The ditch cut me off from the other side. It cut everyone off. No cars could cross and pedestrians lined up to get over a gangplank, two-by-sixes, set end to end for us walkers to navigate. They led from one side of the street, then bridged the ditch and ended up at the far corner on the other side. The pathway was about as wide as my shoe, making crossing a one-way circus act, not a sidewalk jaunt. I waited for a family to come towards me. A little girl in a tutu skirt performed best. The others speed jumped, not relying on balance. I went out, not looking down–well, trying not to–over the ditch. I made a final bolt for the concrete remnant of the old sidewalk on the other side, the one that would be replaced soon. I got there safe, then the next guy behind me started testing his fate.

Crossing had taken up all my thinking. But now, waiting on the corner, I had some spare room upstairs to think about the bakery boys, the spikehairs, the bloody tattoos. Why did Efraím ask about them?

Maybe, better not to think about them.

One more block to my place on the old sidewalk, still full of pot holes and tilted upwards by the trees, but a path

18

I had walked for years and would miss a little when the new street was done.

I walked the last hundred yards, past the shops I knew well. In one doorway I saw Louisa, the woman who cut my hair every month or two. Her three year old played on the floor. She was off in a corner dressing three bald Barbie dolls. The sign said "Tints, Curls, Cuts, Nails, Pedicures." Louisa waved. Her girl ran out and then realizing what she had done, slid back behind the doorway and peered out with one eye just around the doorframe. Then she hid completely again.

A couple of doors up Willy, a fellow expat, walked out of his place and came toward me. We did a quick handshake. I do that with everyone now. You have to do it with the local people and it becomes a habit. Willy, an old-timer, had been here longer than most Mexicans. He arrived during Reagan years. As usual he was off for his stroll in the park. He did not notice much anymore. The city could burn down and he would still take his walk.

Next I passed the *miscelánea*, a store too small to be called a market, stocked with fewer items than a suburban kitchen in the States, with cans neatly lined on shelves, only one or two of each item. Señora Elvira, called out *"hola"* from inside. I said I would be back later for water. Water bottles were part of my daily routine. The new pipes in the street would not make the water any better out of the tap. Tap water was for cleaning and washing. Everyone knew that. So I would her customer forever. I waved goodbye.

Next I passed the little cafe. Comida was later so it was empty. The owner's son, maybe eight or nine, greeted me formally. I wished him a good day and shook his hand. He was growing and wanted a little respect. That was easy to give. Respect is normal down here. Even for a little guy.

The bougainvillea across the street had my eye for a moment and then I looked up at my apartment on the second floor. The balcony was small, but filled with plants. I stuck with geraniums, they grew anywhere, but down here anything grows special if you remember to water it. Mine were half dead of thirst but still pumping out flowers.

I unlocked the small door inset into a larger metal reinforced one–the big swinging one originally used for carts and horses and now for cars. I walked in and passed through the stone outer wall of the building where I lived. I pushed the little door closed–it always stayed closed–and checked the lock. You locked your house here in the city. That was the way it was, where people were poor all around, where most people were good, but many were hungry and might pick up something, and where some were bad. No, they were worse, they were evil. But those were not usually the poor ones. They were the ones who made everyone poor.

Houses here were not white picket fence ones–no green front lawns anywhere. Oaxacan houses descended from castles that Romans and, later, Spanish and their Mexican offspring built with rooms branching inward from the tall thick walls fortifying the property line. A house was built to keep people out.

Inside the walls everything changed. Courtyards opened the center of the building. They breathed in air, grew vines and flowers, and bubbled with old fountains. Courtyards were the gems that made home sweet. They descended from Arab gardens that ruled Spanish leisure for five hundred years and came to Mexico in the dreams of the conquistadors, long after Christians had pushed out, killed or converted everyone in Spain who could not say their rosaries and cross themselves twenty times a day.

Nowadays in the house where I lived, the kids, their dog, and the wash hung out in the courtyard. The family car threatened the fountain and tried to choke out the air, but it was still the garden. Wild-looking flowers bloomed everywhere and a parrot came out to welcome me with a dozen screams.

I walked past María and Lupe. Lupe smiled. They had barely finished doing the wash, with scrub-boards in a cement tank by the fountain. They were the live-in women, the ones who kept everything running, maids for the Señora, the matriarch of the house. María had been there forever. Lupe was recent. I had snatched Lupe back from California—that is part of the reason I am called Santo Gordo.

She ended up pregnant with her boss's baby after she went to *el Norte* to work. Then this wealthy boss locked her up, after he tried to get her to abort Beto, as the baby is now called—short for Roberto—named after me by my landlady, Señora Concepción. She sent me off on that rescue and wanted to reward me. I was still trying to explain to everyone that I was not related. I was the hero, not the father.

I think Lupe was happy back in Oaxaca. The baby was, gurgling in a baby seat next to the clothes tub.

The Señora watched out for these two, overseeing their lives. Their relationship was another Spanish hand-me-down, like the architecture. The descendants of the original people of Mexico now worked for the descendants of the Spanish invaders. The Señora had Spain in her, not pure Spain, but enough. She was erect, pale and tall; María and Lupe were wide, chapped, brown and bent over the washtubs.

Just because the Señora had maids did not mean she was rich, though. She had the house. She had a son and his wife who worked, but not a lot of income, only money from some renters like me. But even though not rich, she, like all her neighbors, had help in the house. She explained that it was her duty to hire those with less. Her servants were not a luxury but a special holy burden. A necessary burden to keep a house and keep her hands clean, a burden that made meals, and continued the life started by the Spanish. Holy was how the Señora saw it as she watched María work and then led her and Lupe to mass every evening. I am not sure how María and Lupe saw it. María did not talk much to me. She smiled and stayed in the background. Lupe laughed, played with the baby and kept trying to hand him to me to hold.

I was going up the stairs when the Señora caught me. I had been expecting it. She knew I went to the *Centro* for my espresso and news traveled fast here for the old residents, as fast as for the young ones with their constant texting. People were on the streets, passing by, exchanging hugs and a word or two about the world. She already knew about the explosion, I was sure. In fact, she probably heard the boom. It was big and only a half mile away.

"*Señor Roberto, gracias a Dios usted está bien.*" My Spanish was getting better. I needed it because she was never going to learn English. She made a point of telling us from the North that Spanish was good enough for her mother and father, so it was good enough for her. And it was the language of God, the one she heard in the church every day, along with Latin, which she thought of as old Spanish.

"*Gracias, Señora, ¿y usted y su familia?*"

Her son and daughter worked far from the dead bakery. The children went to the local school. I knew all was fine. Otherwise the house would have been madness. I did not tell her about the schoolgirls and the donuts, about the spikehaired men, about Efraím's warning. I kept silent.

"*Estamos bien.* We are well, but what a miracle. All were saved. God watches out." She crossed herself a couple of times. I still did not have the crossing motions down. I think you have to learn as a child to do it without thinking like the Mexicans. My crossings have a gringo accent, like my Spanish.

"I hope that it was not part of the problems," she said.

The problems she was thinking of happened some years back. The city revolted, the police and politicians ran away for a while, and then came back with the army. Cars and buses burned. Oaxaca was still recovering.

"Es un milagro. No hubo muertos como antes." No one died this time. She crossed herself again and looked over at her altar to the Virgin. Deep in her heart she knew it was her piety that saved us. She loved her church and the Virgin, like all Mexicans do. Even drug lords and executioners love the Virgin.

We continued through the necessary courtesies when you met someone, even if you had seen them a couple of hours earlier. First asking questions about health and family. This was as necessary as wearing clothes if you wanted to be seen as a real human—not one of those northerners, either Mexican or American, who forgets everything in order to do business, even forgets to slow down for lunch.

I love this place. I always ask about family and I remember my comida. I do not rush, either in greetings and especially in my afternoon meal.

I have become part of the Señora's family, some sort of uncle character who lives at the edges of the family compound, up above the door looking out over the street, walled in, but free to come and go. I feel connected to the family but not so connected that I must go to mass or deal with gossip and family feuds. I did not have those burdens, but I had duties. My role was comfortable, cheery, had meals thrown a couple of times a month. Best, it gave me a window on the non-tourist, non-expat life in the city.

I got through the courtesies and exchanged hugs. I asked after everyone in the family and the dog too. Then business started.

"Remember, *posadas* begin tonight, yes? You will be there?"

This was a polite command, the Señora's type of command.

"Of course, I would not miss it." I was looking forward to the first one, really I was. It was the eight *posadas* that followed, the eight nights of celebration with the family and neighbors singing and marching around the street that wore me down and had me looking for ways to sneak away.

Navidad–Christmas–was coming fast. In Mexico it is not a single holiday. It is a season, like baseball, just about as long but with better fireworks. And not with much shopping. Just a lot of food. Presents come late, after Jesus arrives, about playoff time.

Posadas are the preseason, the nine nights before Christmas when everyone parades around and sings about the pregnant Virgin María, her husband poor José, and his hard-working donkey, all looking for a place to stay. And then everyone gets treats–chocolate and *atole* drinks and tamales.

"Señor Roberto, can you help us for a short time, right now?" the Señora asked nicely.

After finding Lupe in Merced, I had become part of the family, like a not-too-bright child, not fully comprehensible to the Señora. She did know that asking nicely worked well on me, just as inviting me to comida or offering me some tamales or *churros*–that worked, too. I knew she would be offering something when I finished helping. It was like dog training, but tamales are better than dog chews.

I nodded yes to her request. I knew what was coming. She had already started getting ready about a month before the Navidad season with María cooking, and Lupe making candies and cleaning all the decorations. Her son Jorge had taken out his guitar to practice leading the singing at the posada that night. A cousin had started building the room-sized nativity scene with two working waterfalls, a zoo of animals and seven dangling angels.

Right now, she needed someone tall to get the Holy Family down from its place on top of the hutch in the dining room.

Posadas required a procession to be led by the Holy Family, in this case, the Señora's prized, two-foot-tall ceramic sculpture of the Virgin Mary, her husband José and the donkey. I was the tallest in the house, so every year the Señora asked me to get it down.

I climbed onto one of the chairs. It wobbled but held. The Señora's furniture was built to last, probably for a century or two. I reached up over the edge of the hutch–I could not see anything–and got one hand around the Virgin. Ten months of dust rose up in a cloud as I dragged her near the edge. The Señora mouthed prayers asking God to protect the Holy Family. I lifted them–they weighed about twenty pounds–and maneuvered the statue down, cradling Mary to my chest.

Dust fell everywhere. I sneezed but held tight. Lupe tried to help grabbing the donkey's back legs, almost pulling me over, but everything worked out–another miracle. Mary, José, the donkey, and I all descended to earth.

I was getting Catholicized living here. My Protestant brain was drowning in all the Mexican faith and dust. I sneezed again.

I handed the sculpture, intact, to the Señora, feeling a bit winded, maybe dazed, like José must have felt when all this started. The Señora and her Virgin, pregnant, smiling and sitting sidesaddle, were unfazed. They both knew God would take care of things.

Here on earth it was time for the Señora to take care of me.

"Would you like a hot chocolate?" she asked.

Of course, there was no need for an answer. We walked into the kitchen.

María had the clay pot, the *olla*, heating on the stove. Earlier, she had finished kneading the chocolate into a paste, a mix of ground chocolate, seeds, spices–cinnamon, for sure, chilies, and almonds, now ready to drop into the boiling water. No milk was involved, cows came with the Spanish. That would be chocolate sacrilege.

Chocolate is Mexico. Chocolate is a Mayan goddess, *Ixcacao*, who asked for hot drinks, not blood. Emperor Montezuma drank his cupful daily. I was ready for one too.

As the water boiled, María turned the gas to a lower, warming flame and pulled out her wooden *molinillo*–her Mayan-born, hand-carved, chocolate-making spindle. It was nearly a foot tall, wide and bulblike at the bottom, shaped like something I made on a lathe in high school woodworking class years and years ago. It was carved with indentations, niches, and holes, and ringed in the middle with two or three loose fitting hoops, carved from the same

27

piece of wood and trapped on the shaft by a final ridge that had even more slots.

To most gringos it looked like something to shake as you danced around a fire late at night. Maybe at something dead. That just showed how many bad movies we had seen.

María held the *molinillo* loosely in the chocolate-filled *olla*, resting it between her palms. She slid her hands back and forth, spinning it like boy scouts would to start a fire. She went at it for three or four minutes as the niches and rings whipped air into the liquid, frothing it until foam ran over the top. She smiled and poured for me like they did for the Aztecs, holding the pot high over the cup, with the chocolate stream splashing more air into the mixture. A holy art–that was what chocolate making really was. Something like a priest does with wine and water, but better tasting.

I dunked my churro. Mexicans were not sure if dunking was *puro mexicano*, as they say. There is no record of Montezuma doing it, but I had my gringo donut reflex and could not help. Churros, after all, are only long, straight donuts that dunk better than the round ones.

We three were made for each other, my holy trinity–churros, chocolate and me. I was ready to go pagan and worship the chocolate goddess, forget the Virgin, but I could not say that in front of the Señora. Anyway, the chocolate goddess must have converted to Catholicism by now. Everything preconquest was fair game for the holy men in black robes. Sometimes I expected to see Jesus sporting a headdress doing the Aztec stomp in the Zócalo, sipping from a big chocolate-filled cup. The church had put a Catholic wrapping around everything here. Even me. I was Santo Gordo, after all.

María poured the Señora's and then the cups for herself and Lupe. I had come first that day. Not the normal order of things. My drink went fast. I am not a sipper. The Señora smiled and looked toward María. She frothed up some more, poured and added a pair of fat churros to my plate. Yes, heaven dips close to earth on some days.

Of course, it was pretty far away that morning when the bakery blew.

We sat around the table in the kitchen. The Señora wanted to remind everyone about the morning miracle at the bakery and the new flowers on her altar. She was doing her holy instruction to the women and me. It was starting to take a little on me. I could tell because I did not jump any more when they called me Santo. But I did when they got to Gordo.

****

I got my biggest straw hat and darkest sunglasses—it was noon and the sun was high. Mary and the her Holy Family had been placed in the shade on the terrace. I would be out in the street. The temperature would only touch 85 that day, but the sun burned hot in Oaxaca during the afternoon. The city is a mile high and about as far south as I ever want to go. The sun bakes everything, but gringos most of all. Then it runs off and leaves you alone with the cold, tall mountains. The climate seems crazy to everyone from the States. Tour books call it an endless spring, but not a US one. In Oaxaca, spring is hot, summer is wet, winter is dry, and fall is when they celebrate the Day of the Dead, sitting out in graveyard during the cool evening.

Oaxaca had been dry for a month, like normal in the winter. Mosquitos were dead, puddles were gone, dust rose up with the slightest stir of the wind, and everything that needed water had died. I would too if I forgot my hat and got cooked in the streets.

I kept thinking about the bakery and the two spikehairs that I met earlier that day, as I stooped and walked out the little door in the wall of the house. Those two were not there for pastries, that was for sure. But I did not notice much about them. Finding out more was not a job for Santo Gordo. I retired from crime fighting last year, if that is what you want to call it when I bumbled into a killing.

I decided to walk up the big hill today, to work up an appetite for lunch after the hot chocolate, and to forget about the morning. Walking does that, especially when it takes your breath away. I was huffing after a couple of blocks, even before I reached the stairway.

Oaxaca lies flat in a high valley surrounded by mountains. One of them nestles right up to the Centro, not a big one, maybe just a hill, but big enough for all the TV towers, along with a planetarium and a big outdoor amphitheater that sits like a monument or temple up on top.

A thousand-foot-long stone and cement stairway climbs the hill. I looked up the stairs from the other side of the final street before the steps started, waited for the line of buses to chug past, then I ran across like a rabbit, well, a slow rabbit, through a break in the traffic and got to the other curb. This was going to be work.

The stairway was another Oaxacan miracle. It led straight up the hillside, on a pathway lined with houses and trees, uninterrupted by city streets. Nothing crossed the stairs. Streets wove left and right at the side of the stairs. The streets had evolved from staggering oxcart and burro lanes that wound their way to the top, but the stairs were an engineer's doing, with no turns to slow the ascent. I climbed twenty steps to the first landing. A dozen or so landings waited in front of me. I would pace myself and stop and look around every hundred feet. I would be hungry after this, or happily dead, overcome by beauty and lack of oxygen.

I passed by trees lining the steps, ones dating back to the revolution. They covered the walkway with a thick, green, shade that rose to block out the sky and the view much of the time, but kept us older climbers from sunstroke. A breeze moved slowly up the hill. It was dry and warm, but took away some of the sweat and cooled down the armpits and everywhere else dripping after a landing or two.

People going down were not straining. They chatted in groups or had their cell phones out. Young kids going up ran past me laughing at the one-step-at-a-time guy. Maids in long aprons doing errands, carrying baskets on their heads passed me. Even wiry old men passed me. But that was OK. I was in no hurry. Lunch was still an hour away.

I came upon a dozen students carrying backpacks, trudging even more slowly than I, on their way to afternoon school sessions, walking like they had been sentenced to a dozen years' hard labor. Then a pair of tourists passed, clacking their high tech walking sticks, peering out, half hidden by their sunhats, a cross between old puritan bonnets and an over-engineered sunshade. We all proceeded up or down, sometimes greeting each other, sometimes head down and breathing hard. I was one of the breathers.

I made it up the first half. Rough wooden booths sat on the landing there. Kids sold soft drinks, chewing gum and candy. Just ahead, one house had a table sitting next to the steps offering tamales and cerveza and a bathroom. I was too sweated out for the bathroom. I thought about the beer but kept on.

Houses by the steps were getting spruced up. Buyers from the north, both from the States and upper Mexico, were taking over. Hip new owners lived a new style, supplied by SUVs, not like the old days when servants ran up and down the steps with food, drinks, and everything else.

I kept climbing, finally reaching the last landing. Up ahead, thirty more steps and through the tunnel under the highway to the plaza in front of the amphitheater, the one used mostly for the yearly folkloric dance festival. Recently, though, you could see lasers and floodlights shooting up from pop shows every month or so. Things were changing.

I went up the final steps and then after getting to the plaza, looked back down the hill. The panorama was the reason tourists climbed, except for crazy joggers who just turned around at the top and ran back down without looking. You could see the whole city below–churches, squares, parks, markets, people, bus stations, everything. And cars. They were everywhere. That was the difference from the time when I arrived in Oaxaca. The streets were emptier then.

The mountains on the other side of the city were topped with two perfect white clouds, the kind a theater director would have painted on his backdrops. I watched the city half an hour. The sun moved a little and I sweated more. It was worth it. Then I was hungry and ready to go back down to eat.

But first, I walked over to the statue of Oaxaca's favorite son, Benito Juarez, the President of Mexico back when Lincoln was running the States. I gave Benito a salute. He deserved it. He stood fifty feet tall up on his pedestal and looked down sternly reminding me to do my duty, as he had done. I said maybe and then I turned back towards the stairs.

Then I saw them, the two spikehair guys standing in the parking lot by the plaza. Talking with someone Mexican in a suit. I moved back behind Benito's feet and tried not to look at the conversation going on. They probably would not recognize me. I was just another big, old, short-bearded gringo. I put on my tourist face and turned my head back out over the city.

They crossed the lot and moved over to the line of cars parked there. I think some lovemaking and low-end drug deals go down in this spot. The guidebooks say be careful at night. Broken glass crunched when they walked. I could hear it a hundred feet away. The suit got in his car and drove off. After a minute or two, my two got into an old sedan. It was the type you see a lot here. Older than the driver, it looked like it had a hard life. Maybe out in a village, where dirt roads and pot holes rule over anything four-wheeled. I always thought the gangs down here had big SUVs with dark windows. I wondered whether their car even had windows.

They pulled out like they wanted to leave fast, throwing gravel at a car coming into the parking lot. They picked up speed going down the ramp back towards to the highway.

A couple of cabs were sitting close to me in the lot.

"Follow that car." I pointed at the sedan. It did not slow down at the stop sign turning on to the highway. This was like the movies.

"We don't follow people, we go places. Tell us where you want to go." The first driver looked over at his friend like they were dealing with someone a little off. Maybe I was. I was a dog on a chase.

The second driver looked at me. "That's Santo Gordo, Efraím's friend. Maybe you ought to do it."

Efraím had a lot of pull these days now that he had his new cab and everyone heard about how he worked with Santo Gordo to save the village. The truth was Efraím did the work and I was the gordo.

"If you want, you do it." The first cabbie was not in a mood to chase anything. He probably had seen the guys in the parking lot looking like gangsters, or drug guys, or both."

His friend told me, "Get in, but in the back. There are a thousand cabs, but not so many with an old gringo in the front. I don't want them to notice me."

I was coming to my senses a little and started to think about what I was doing. I was about to say forget it when the first driver pushed me in the rear seat of his friend's cab and signaled for him to take off.

"Stay low. I'll take care of this."

I did the chase looking at the door handle of a Nissan. Then the floor pad. We started out fast, but the driver slowed abruptly and made a sharp turn. Then we doubled back on the highway toward my part of the city and headed down the hill.

"Do not worry. They are up ahead and a bunch of cabs are between us. Look invisible and I will do everything else. I am an expert. I used to hunt deer up in the pueblo. That is much harder. Deer pay attention—these guys just play loud music."

It was true. I could hear the tubas and the thumping beat from pretty far away. Even on the floor in the back of a cab.

It seemed time to introduce myself to the driver. "Call me Roberto. That's my name." I did not want to be called Santo Gordo any more.

"OK, Santo."

His name was Raul. He started talking how he used to live in a village near Efraím. Then he was in the States, but he came back and got married. He had lots of family, like everyone. It was a nice conversation. Not what I expected in a car chase. It did not seem to slow him down. I was thrown all around the back so I figured he was lead-footing while he talked. Then he stopped.

"The traffic is a jam," Raul explained. "I am ten cars back."

So I told him just a little about me while we sat there. It seemed like the thing to do. "I got old and came here to get warm. I stayed." He seemed happy and started singing. The meter was clicking away, keeping time.

I had forgotten about money. Someone has to pay for this type of thing. No one pays in the movies. In real life you hope you only pay money, not blood.

We drove ten more minutes, mostly straight at first but then turning, with lots of long traffic stops. He called out street names as we passed. I knew them—we passed through the center of the city.

He stopped. "I am not going farther. The men stopped one block over. By an old hotel, the kind that people from the country stay in. No toilet paper, no towels, no bottled water, not even a bathroom on every floor, none of the things you gringos like. You can walk if you want, but I have to stay alive. I do not follow this type very closely."

"Let's just drive back to the Zócalo." I was done with the chase. We passed the spikehaired guys' hotel.

Raul got on the radio and told everyone that he had Santo Gordo on a secret mission. That probably was not the best thing to do. But he was not one of the strong silent types, like Efraím, like the type I was trying to be.

"You have a surprise," He said after he got off the radio. I looked out the window and saw Efraím sitting there in his cab, right in front of me.

"Roberto, get in, we have to talk," Efraím shouted to me. I squeezed out of one back seat and eased into the front seat of my friend's cab.

"Welcome, my detective friend, I must tell you, you still do not know how to keep quiet. I heard the radio talking with you."

"I saw the men from the bakery and got carried away. You know how life is. It surprises you."

"I know how death is. It surprises, too. But you gringos must follow an impulse–Americans are supposed to follow the money, but you are different. You follow gangsters. "

"But I found them…."

"Señor Roberto, it is time to step back and think about life a little. First, you must think of yourself not as a single being, but as a man on a horse."

Efraím liked to think of himself as a philosopher taxista, but one from the country. Whenever he wanted to tell me something he put on his philosopher sombrero. His philosophy was full of horses, beans and often needed rain.

"When you go forward, you must sit high in the saddle, look carefully ahead and guide the horse. The horse, she looks at the ground and she stops for a clump of grass, she runs when she hears a loud sound, or a gangster scream."

I laughed. "The only thing I know about horses is which end to feed. I look for teeth." Efraím was leading me somewhere with his horse–it was best to wait. If I pushed ahead, then he would just invoke Mexicano privilege–that was what he called it–getting to the point by any route he wanted.

"Let me start again. I will explain, in a special gringo version of my story. You, Roberto, are like a rich American man with a dog. This man wants to cross the park. He knows what he needs. An espresso in a restaurant on the other side. But the dog goes for anything, a smell, another dog, even an old tortilla wrapping. Roberto, you must take control and pull the dog back. The dog is the part of Roberto who wants to be a detective and follow any scent. Do not follow these urges of your detective nose without planning ahead. Your detective needs a strong leash. Your urges will not get you old tortillas like the dog. They will get you a bullet, or worse." Efraím was laughing.

I could not keep quiet. "I found where they stay…"

"Everyone knew where they stayed. All the taxistas knew. Why they stayed is what I wanted to know. And now, I think I know after this happened, maybe money on top of the stairs, where you were watching."

"They got money? I followed the wrong one?"

"No, you did not know who to follow because you had no plan. That was the problem. Remember we do not have the luxury of getting carried away down here. We only get carried away when we die. Now go eat your comida. I wish I could go with you today and talk more. And remember hold the leash tight on your dog detective. Let us start planning this tomorrow. I need your help."

Efraím was not angry. He wanted me to help. This was more than his normal philosopher's lecture. He was scared, I think. For me and for him too. But it was his kind of scared, one that had him laughing. And he wanted me to help him. I was ready. Life was getting way too interesting.

38

Something needed to be done, with a plan. But this was Mexico. We would wait until tomorrow.

Efraím slapped me on the back. "I know in el Norte you have an inner child, or maybe an inner dog. But we cannot allow ourselves an inner creature that does not think hard, even an inner detective. Our inner being is only for holding food."

His radio blurted and Efraím yelled into the mike, "*Momento, ya me voy.* I am leaving." He turned back to me. "I must go. Tomorrow, meet me for comida and we decide what to do, like old times when we got shot at and saved Mexico."

"I did not save Mexico, I barely saved my neck."

I sat alone at a table in the Zócalo worried someone was watching after my wild thug chase. Maybe the spikehairs themselves. Their hotel was not that far away. That thought took away a little hunger at first, not much, but enough. Then I kept thinking about the people sitting around, the ones who had heard Efraím and me talking, wondering what we were doing. But it was time for comida. Time to put away worrisome things. This was Mexico.

I ate a little. That made me hungrier. Then I ate a lot. I stopped seeing thugs everywhere. I saw only tamales, looking lifeless but happy, flopped down on the plate, sticking out their corn *masa* edges up over their husk wrappers. One *tamal* reached out of the *mole* sauce, asking for help, the other swam in the salsa verde, the green sauce, having fun. I helped myself, sliced one open and did an autopsy. Steamed to death–that was the verdict–then drowned with sauce to cover the evidence.

39

My comida was more than a meal. It was a meditation. No words, only tastes and chews. I ate one tamal. I slugged at the cerveza. Then I focused on the chicken thigh and the tamal in the other sauce, the hot green one with an acid taste and a big zing, squeezed from tomatillos. The chicken soaked everything in, like my stomach was doing. I sopped up with the tortillas. Then I finished off the black beans and rice. I was at peace. My plate in life was clean.

To end it all, I ordered espresso. Then I was complete.

I looked up. The *Zócalo* had grown darker while I ate. Or maybe it was me—my eyes were closing. Things were fuzzy. Time for a nap, part of my ongoing, old man training. I staggered out, overfilled, and got a cab home.

****

"Time for the Posada." Lupe yelled up to me. I moved a little in my bed. Her baby screamed. I opened my eyes. The room was dark. Nap was over. I was groggy but coming around. The food had worked its way down. That was good. Food sins are like the rest. They are forgiven here in Mexico, and you are expected to get up and try again. I was ready. Ready to go greet the Virgin Mary in her pre-Christmas, highly pregnant fiesta.

No fancy clothes were required for the posada, just clean ones, so I washed up a little and snipped the mustache and beard. Then headed down to the courtyard.

The whole neighborhood was already there. The Señora had brought out the family. The women stood on one side and her oldest son was there with his guitar. She was too busy to look my way. She guided everyone, as we got ready to find the Virgin Mary a place to stay for the night. That was what the posadas were—looking for a place to stay. Like some of the tourists who came for Christmas and did not make reservations.

I get all the kids mixed up. There are children of all sorts of relations, with connections that take a paragraph to describe in English but only a word or so in Spanish. Spanish likes family and has words for it. English has hyphens—daughter-in-law, cousin-twice-removed. Relations like that. Gringo men never learn these things right in Spanish. We have hyphenating in our brains. That makes it easier to cut relations. Just snip the little dash. Down here, in Spanish, it is harder.

Some cousins from near D.F.—what they call the capital of Mexico—had come and one family had flown in from LA for three weeks. Families from *pueblitos* around Oaxaca were here. Families from across the street, too. The posadas were part of neighborhood life. You knew everyone. They all knew about you. There were no invitations, just the word round the block. The invite was in your *buenos días* in the church or on your way shopping for a chicken or some tortillas around the corner at the little shop everyone goes to.

One boy handed out xeroxed sheets of paper with the posada prayers and songs while another handed out sparklers—one per person. There was a free-for-all for the tambourines. Everybody wanted one. I had brought my own down from my room. I was prepared and ready to shake it.

The crowd got bigger. More neighbors and families showed up. Some of the older people dressed like on a Sunday trip, but most just wore their day clothes. Tourists and expats who knew the Señora were there. The women tourists wore Oaxacan handmade shawls and *rebozos,* and some of the men had Mexican shirts with fancy embroidery. They played born-again Mexican. I did not–I wore fake Dockers and stood in the back.

The guitar started with a melody and added some chords. The Señora started with commands to the women. They sang. The men joined in. I went an octave under and died on the low notes but plugged away beating the tambourine on my thigh. Like in a crowd at a rock concert, but without the rock.

Then we prayed some. The Señora led. Finally, after ten minutes of *Kyries* and *Fili Redemptors* and other Catholic mysteries to us Protestant-born and Latin-free, one of the grandchildren picked up the statue, the pregnant Virgin Mary, José and the donkey, the one I had taken down earlier. The one I got my hot chocolate reward for. The one that lived all year on the top of the high dresser waiting for these nights.

The statue led us. The boy carried it carefully, looked left and right, and stepped forward slowly. Family women walked behind. Everyone else followed.

As we got to the door at the street, two older boys held burning sparklers. We touched our unlit ones, mating them with ones already burning until ours too sputtered into a hot bright light, the kind you could weld with. Everyone passed by the lighting station and got their sparkler going. Most just waved it a little, making flares and wiggles as they walked and sang heading into the street. A few adults, mostly gringo visitors, and all the children made swooping circles and slashes, writing their names and drawing animal shapes with their sparklers, burning words and pictures into their eyeballs.

I tried not to trip on the doorway, looking past the holes and streaks in my vision, blanked out by the white-hot sparkler glare that ate holes into my view.

I tried not to walk in front of a child. Kids were not careful. I had a hole or two in my shirts to show where they had bumped, fire first, into my back. Last year I had a round burn mark, just right for a tortured saint, but everything had healed by the time Navidad came around again.

A rocket hissed, and its red streak rose from one of the workmen's hands a few feet in front of the procession. It exploded directly overhead. Car alarms went off on both sides of the street. Burning paper debris fell slowly, gliding from side to side, usually extinguishing itself completely as it dropped down on our heads and fell underfoot. But some still glowed on the ground. Sometimes up in the hills when people marched their posada there, it lit the grass on fire.

Another rocket was launched. The singing got louder. We blocked cars and trucks in the road. Mostly, they waited silently. This was a posada and we had priority. I walked in the crowd about half way back and looked up at the night sky waiting for another rocket. Orion and his belt were up there too, like they were every year, waiting for baby Jesus to get born.

We continued around the block. The procession was not something that had to be planned. Everyone had done this since they could walk, even before, carried by mothers, and then later, by sisters and cousins and fathers, following the Virgin as she looked for her Christmas night out. Everyone knew the song. Everyone knew the prayers. Everyone knew the route, past the church, a quick right, and then back a block and up a little, returning to the front door of the Señora's house.

We passed the church. The crowd had grown. All the neighbors were there now, or at least all that wanted to show the Señora some Christmas good will. That was most of them. And a few more tourists wandering by had joined in. They were welcome. You could tell them in the dark by their camera flashes. They acted like this was something special that might not happen again, something they had never seen before–it probably was. And they sang too. The song had a chorus everyone could sing. Tourists did not sing real words, but something like la la-la-la. Sort of like I sang.

Every fifty feet another rocket went up. Another set of car alarms joined in. Christmas was noisy. Not just a hundred untrained voices, not just the guitar and the tambourines that everyone pounded and jingled, but also the Señora's booming voice as she got serious about her religion

Finally we arrived in front of the house. The Señora and some older women went inside and closed the door while most of us stayed out. The boy with the statue sat the Virgin Mary and her family down on a table by the entrance. She needed to rest after all the explosions and noise. I was ready to rest a little, too.

We started singing again. This was the begging song. "Let me in, let me in." I remembered some of the Spanish words and belted them out. I belted the tambourine. I was glorious.

"Give us some shelter, my wife cannot travel, let us in." The women inside the door answered. "This is not a hotel. You look like a crook."

We dueled with our verses a dozen times. My favorite was "I am a carpenter, I am tired. I am José." With the answer "I don't care. Get lost. Let me sleep."

The night would have ended for me right there with me slamming the door, if I were the innkeeper, but José goes on and on and wears everyone out, finally saying Mary, the Queen of Heaven, is with him. God is going to pay for it all. That gets the gates open.

I wanted to try that in hotels around Christmas time. God had not paid up for a while—that was one of our problems. Or maybe it was better if he stayed away and let us be.

Anyway we finally got in the door after the Señora and her team opened it when we finished our final begging verse. We prayed some more. We did *Our Fathers* and *Ave Marias*.

Then we sang the big finale thanking the godmother of the posada, the Señora, the person who paid for everything, for the sparklers and the soon-to-come food and candy. *"Hola madrina, sal de la cocina con la canasta de gelatina"*—"Hey, Godmom, get out of the kitchen, and bring that basket filled with goodies."

Then the globalization twist comes in. The final line asks for a Coca-Cola. I don't know who added that, but it had been there since I got to Mexico.

The Coke marketing people had put a Christmas tree in the park, too, the year before. It was hung with colored Coke bottles. Of course that was when the president of Mexico was an ex-marketing guy from the Coke Company. El Norte was sneaking, or maybe pouring, into the deep south of Mexico. Christmas was fair game.

The Señora got the message. She went into her room and came out leading her son and daughter, all carrying baskets filled with candy. I got one of the chocolate-covered clowns on a stick, mostly marshmallow and a mess. That was fine with me. This was Christmas, a messy time of the year.

The party ended with hot drinks and a snack—tamales wrapped in banana leaves, steamed, some goopy and greasy with *mole* sauce and chicken meat dripping out the middle and some with raisins and sweets. All made of corn mush—*masa*, they call it. It could absorb any kind of sauce. The perfect plop of carbos holding the fat and meat and spices together. *Mole* tamales had a glow-in-the-dark orange seeping into the masa. The sweet ones had a day-glow pink. God knows what was in it, but God's secrets never got in my way. I flipped the banana leaves open and dug out the hearts of the tamales like some starved lion going after a Christian. Christmas brings out the best in me.

The Señora came around to the tables set up in the street and in the courtyard, all full of people eating away. She greeted us like some old preacher or salesman back home. She was doing her job, the job she loved, running the neighborhood. And yes, you could take over a street if you wanted for a party. Traffic always came second.

Then five or six rockets announced everything was done. I was done, for sure. A couple of drinks and four drippy tamales. What a night.

****

I had been on good behavior during the posada the night before—one beer. OK, it was two—but no mezcal, and lots of masa mush to absorb everything. No hangover. No food locked in an acid-eaten stomach bubbling away like sometimes.

I woke up shining. The sun was up, too. We were going together for my espresso, me in a hat and shades, the sun bareheaded and looking over the mountains down at Oaxaca with a big smile.

I grabbed yesterday's clothes. The pants had rumples, but I was a gringo. Mexicans gave us some style slack as long as we did not wear cargo shorts and sandals. Or those devil pants, those skinny jeans for men.

I can be fast when my caffeine alarm goes off. Getting dressed took a minute. The alarm was ringing hard that day, and I knew only one way to shut it off, a double espresso. Maybe a triple, if the alarm was really loud.

I made it down the stairs unnoticed. In the mornings I was a sneak. Getting caught was agony because there were no short conversations in stairwells if you ran into the Señora. I would have visions of coffee beans while she had ones of God as she gave me a long-version morning blessing.

I cut behind the parked car in the courtyard and out the little door to the street. My only conversation that morning was going to be with my stomach.

I had a lot planned for the day–first, get a donut and espresso and, later, plot something secret with Efraím.

I was going to be unfaithful. My old espresso joint would not care, I hoped. A new espresso bar had opened next to my number-two bakery. Number one was gone, blown up.

I headed north, not towards "La Avenida," my normal morning kickstart for the past year or two, but towards the German bakery and its neighbor, the chrome and glass place with stainless steel everywhere, looking clean enough for surgery, not espresso.

I walked past the pumpernickel and pretzels looking for the hot, sweet dough twisty things, gooey and covered with enough sugar and chocolate to get me into a fit. Then I went over to the new espresso place next door–bar stools, good Italian roaster, grinder, and steam pump. Nice *crema*. I got my double and did a fat dunk. Two minutes flat and I was me. My ears were buzzed. Five minutes and I had a great caffeine twitch.

I had not noticed Carlos while I was drowning everything in the espresso. I do not notice much before my cup is empty. Carlos used to be a Charles. But no one local could pronounce that tricky English name, so he became a Carlos.

He waved over to me. "Roberto, *buen día.*"

I had done the Mexican name switch, too. I used to be Robert Evans, but everyone called me Roberto. I had no choice but I liked it. A lot better than Santo Gordo.

He stood in the corner, chatting up some local guys in suits. Everyone Mexican wore their suit uniform after they made a certain grade of management. Sometimes with a vest but always a coat and tie. Carlos wore his suit too, but as a memory. He tried to look business but was rumpled and had sandals. To be business you needed a shoeshine, one out in the park from the pros in their roll-in shoeshine stands. Carlos wanted too much, both business and air between his toes.

He was retired, but like most old expats, needed a little more dough to be comfortable. In some cases comfort meant nothing more than not sharing a bathroom with five or six people. Carlos was a step above that. He had an apartment, a nice terrace to look out from, but for him, like for everyone, things got shaky if something out of the ordinary hit you, a necessary quick flight home or some down time getting repaired in the hospital. He was running month to month. Uncle Sam does provide when you get to 65, but only the basics. Carlos was living the same as me, same as a lot of expats. Our daily bread and not much more.

That day, he had his shark smile. He was prowling.

"Roberto, *buen día*." He repeated his greeting. "I have been looking for you." He pulled his tie loose. That was his gringo business style. It hung down in the front. A sparse ponytail dropped over his collar in the back. He had the Arizona look, or maybe the Mexico beach look. Sun is good for lots of things, but not skin. He was sunned out and looked like a lizard in a suit.

My generation did not save our skins. We Euro-Americans peeled off God-knows-how-many skin layers and hoped any newborn cancer cells came off with the rest. But we have learned. We wear hats now. And after 65 years of getting radiated, we use sun cream for bad days, say, when we are out at noon—no one does that much—or up at the ruins, a thousand feet nearer the sun, with some tourista relatives who have come on vacation and want a free guide. They want a tan to die for, one to show off when they go home.

Mexicans do not use sun cream. They have it built-in. We don't. Because up in Europe, living in dark caves for generations and generations while the ice ages raged, we lost our built-in sunblockers. We killed off all the mastodons, wiped out the Neanderthals, and lost our tans. Now we try to get them back in two weeks.

Carlos and I did our saludos, the handshake part but not the hugs. I save those for my Mexican friends. He had his coffee—he was a watery drinker, with a lot of milk. And not a dunker. That was why he kept skinny. He smiled again. I knew something was coming.

"I know you don't like the Santo Gordo thing. I mean, those bad guys came after you a while back, didn't they?"

I never talked Santo Gordo to anyone. No one knew about what really had happened the year before when I got messed up with Efraím's village and the government. I kept it that way. I stared down at the empty cup. And the left-over chocolate smear. I needed more.

"Another double," I called out to the barista behind the pump.

Carlos patted me on the back. He always did this when he hatched something.

"You know what you need? An agent. An agent for Santo Gordo. I could sell your story and you could make a bunch. Expat gets in trouble, expat gets in more trouble, expat gets out of trouble. What a story. You just have to fill in the details."

"I don't write. My details are boring. I just live here. I don't do trouble." Sometimes it is harder than others to be trouble-free. I did not tell Carlos this. He would tell me that would sound great on the cover.

I looked up from my cup at him. He used to be a lawyer. Probably not a good one or he would be living up the hill with the rich gringos and the Mexican politicians.

"Roberto, who needs the true story? I am talking about a book, a mystery, one set in Oaxaca. It will sell itself. Of course, your life is boring. But don't tell it that way."

"I don't tell anything, anyway. I want to live here." My emphasis was on the live part. The alternative was not live somewhere else–it was die. You kept some things quiet. Not only here, everywhere.

I was done talking. My double was on the way. I needed to get him moving. "Charles, if you want a story, you have to make it up yourself."

I Charles'd him, I did that to Mister Carlos when his time was up.

"I might. You just might see Santo Gordo in your bookstore one day."

I think that was a threat. I did not care. Carlos did not do much of what he started. The double espresso arrived. And the barista brought a *pan dulce*, a *concha*. That is the fat round pastry with gooky sugar on the top. My dunking would keep going a while.

"Thanks for the offer, Carlos. If I decide to write it down, you will be the first to hear."

"Good, I'll keep checking."

He did not get my message, my no. This was Mexico and you did not put a rejection big and up front like in the States–you said it in small letters and were polite. I had learned this with Mexican friends and it spilled over on my Americans.

Carlos checked the time. We shook hands–you have to shake after meeting, that was the Mexican rule with anyone, probably even with the devil. Carlos took off and I was staring down at the rest of the pastry. Thinking about what I had to do that day–nothing. Except see Efraím and plan something. He always had something going, something interesting, something way too interesting for an expat like me. But I would go to see him later.

The caffeine wanted action. I wanted rest. I had a couple of hours so I went back to the apartment and took a nap to get ready.

****

Nap was over. It was time. Efraím had said comida and he would pick me up. He was out front.

"What's happening?" I asked.

He just smiled and said, "You will see. This is something special for you."

I have learned that when life does not answer your questions immediately, let life alone for a couple of days. The same applied to Efraím.

I watched the road as we drove along. We were heading out towards the new shopping area. First, we passed the big Mormon temple. It was trying to compete with the cathedral but was fenced in. Those Mormons would have to open it up to the public if they really wanted to take over Mexico. A church is a public space down here. One with music, hot dogs, dancing music, masked wrestling, drama, and fireworks. I don't know if the Mormons can take that. Especially with rockets blasting over their angel, like the Catholics do for Jesus.

We passed the university. The architecture school was modern, low and rectangular, like something southwest. The rest was cement, utilitarian, and just past ugly, but it was alive. The grounds had trees and walls painted over

53

with political slogans. Students milled around near the food trucks announcing loads of *tortas* and hamburgers.

You never knew what was going to happen on campus—students struck, unions struck, nonstudents struck because they were not admitted. Student life was complicated, a lot more so than in the States where the only real complication was money. Or maybe I had forgotten all the other ones. But there were no strikes these days in the States. Just post-school job fear and interview anxiety.

We went by a five-story cement office building. It stood out. Somehow it passed height restrictions and towered over everything. Other buildings had a thrown-together, one-story look, lining the road with shops. The big cement one was for business, maybe for government, a look into the future of Oaxaca. Its windows did not open, and the power went off often. It would be a hot future.

We passed beauty salons, internet cafes and, tire stores, with some new tires and a lot used. We passed print shops that cranked out 4 by 6 foot posters for your business or your protest. We passed a dozen small family places to eat tacos and chicken. We passed a Domino's Pizza with a crowd of dented but shined motorcycles, little guys—50ccs with big metal pizza boxes welded on the back. They lined up in the street, ready to go. Like soldiers waiting for an inspection, or leading an invasion.

We passed car dealers selling *semi-nuevos*—the used car catchword down here. Then we came to the shopping centers with copies of American malls on the right, a Sears, a Cineplex, a French department store and a big Mexican one too—a downscale Target. Then on the left was the

Sam's Club. And up the street the new Walmart. This was the new Mexico after NAFTA. It was a great treaty for businesses going south and bad for little guys on both sides of the border. Unless they wanted to be clerks or stockboys. Maybe they did. Most thought it was a lot better than nothing.

This was the new Oaxaca of big parking lots. Along with SUVs and weekly bargains with coupons. We expats could not get used to it–it violated all our dreams of Mexico–but the middle class here was happy. And the middle class was the new Mexico–that was what the newspapers said. You might believe it, too, if you stayed in the center of the city and saw the cars and new ten-wheeled, high-tech baby strollers prowling the streets. Before NAFTA, kids walked and babies got wrapped against their mamas in a *rebozo*. That was old Mexico.

Do not get me wrong–old Mexico was not dead. More poor Oaxacans than ever were born each day and the essence of old Mexico was poverty, a poverty that lived a home-grown, home-made, home-cooked life, the opposite of the disposable import world of the new middle class. There was going to be more than enough poverty to go around for a long time.

We kept going. The road became a highway. It ran down to the coast a hundred miles and eight hairpin-curve hours away. It also went by the airport.

"Are you shipping me off? Are we going to the airport?"

"I would not let you sneak away, Señor Gordo. I need to ask you something. I just wanted to get away, in case anyone was watching and listening. I think we have shaken anyone following us. He turned into a roadside chicken stand–a grill and a lean-to house made of corrugated metal propped up on a wall of unmortared bricks. Ready for the next earthquake, ready to fall over and squash someone.

"Hola, Rodrigo," Efraím seemed to know everyone. I had no idea where we were. Efraím put his arm around a man about my age. A thin, weathered man with veins in his arms bigger than my muscles. Work can do that to you.

"This is my Tío Rodrigo. He is a businessman. He cooks chickens." Everyone was a businessman when there were no jobs.

The older man grabbed my hand. He led us to a table and some plastic chairs. This was his life, his business as Efraím had said. I looked at the chickens out behind the wall. They were in business too. The leg and egg business. They were going to make a sale. I was hungry.

Efraím did the formal intros. Everyone *saludo*'d and did a *mucho gusto*. I was now a friend, once removed.

Efraím and I sat and ate—chicken and beer, with some salsa to make it Mexican.

Then he started in on me. Tío knew not to listen. This looked like Efraím's business office. The chickens would not spy on us. We were secure.

"It's bad." I waited for more. Efraím was thinking. I was thinking that he never took a break driving taxi during the day. He never took a free drive. He never did what he did today. So I knew it was bad.

"They are after my other uncle, Tío Francisco. He would not sell to them."

This was too cryptic for me. But Efraím had never talked much about his troubles before—he said it was to keep me pure and innocent. But I thought it was so I would not blab it around. Today was new ground.

"They blew up his place. They threatened and told him to sell the building. Sell it right away. Someone wanted to buy it. Then they saw a chance for a bigger threat. The hose with propane hung down from the roof, right in front of my uncle, right by the door with the two men looking at the hose swinging back and forth, as the truck was pumping propane up to the tank on the roof. They slashed it. The two men you saw with tattoos slashed it. My uncle ran to the back and got everyone out. He yelled and the bakers ran."

Efraím took a deep breath—he looked like some windup animal that had run down. He slugged at his cerveza, shook his head, and continued, "The gas did not seep out the cut hose. It sprayed out and then, in five minutes, with everyone across the street, it exploded. My uncle called me, and I sent him to the hospital. He was not far enough away. He was watching the front window where your donuts lived. He was burned and he was cut. But why would they blow up a building they wanted to buy?"

Now I knew what had happened. I knew too much—I knew something I could never get free of. Like a chain around my neck. Because I was sure other people knew I knew. Efraím looked pained. He knew a lot more than me.

"I could have killed those two. But I needed to know. And now they are gone—no one knows where they are—maybe dead. Not by me. I think because they are stupid.

They were hired to buy the building. Instead, they blew it up. Stupid."

"They might be dead? Because they screwed up?" I was learning way too much.

"I think so. They disappeared. Someone wanted the buildings because of gringos coming here. Gringos with too much money. I can take care of the *Mexicanos* involved, but they are like fish being fed from above, and if a rotten one gets yanked out by the hook, then another takes its place. Money on a hook is strong bait. I want us to work together. I scare the Mexicans. You scare the gringos, the ones with the hooks up north." He looked at me.

"Scare the Americans?" I said mostly to myself. I am not very scary, except to a donut.

Efraím looked up towards God somewhere in the sky. "I will scare the Mexicans maybe to death." That was the last thing he said for a while.

The Mexicans should be scared. Efraím had more than just the eyes of hundreds of cab drivers in Oaxaca, he had their fists and knives and sometimes, I think, guns. He was big in the taxista union, a union tied into the government, yes, the same union that sometimes sets up barricades against the government. But they were linked. As Efraím always told me. "It is complicated."

People knew the taxistas had power. They had the ears of the powerful. They had a free hand late at night. I had tried not to know this. But I knew deep down, and now I knew even more.

A while back, one of the taxistas got locked up in a police station right outside of town. In minutes a hundred taxi drivers raided the police station, beat up the police, and carried the guy out. Police did nothing. Now the guy is on vacation on the coast. He was Efraím's friend.

Power shows itself down here. Not like in the States where power is layered with lawyers and lobbyists and law book rituals secret to most of us. Power is never a secret in Mexico; it walks upright all around you. It carries rifles in pickups. You can see it if you are not buried in your guidebook or staring up at churches. You can see it, and it can see you. Except maybe in a chicken restaurant run by your uncle, way out on the highway to the coast.

****

Efraím dropped me off back in town. We had a deal. I was not sure exactly what it was. But I was going north soon, after the holidays. I would figure out what to do up there, how to act scary to the money guys later on.

I had an hour or two before posada number two with the Señora. I stopped in La Avenida for a quick hit. Just a single, with some *espuma*, foam. I sipped, not my style, but I wanted to look down the street at the bakery through the new window at La Avenida. The bakery was still pink but had soot overlaying the color. It still had window frames with glass shards, sharp and pointed, wedged in the rails and looking dangerous. Someone had covered the wall with sheets of corrugated sheet metal, but it had holes in it. I needed to see more.

No one was in the building. I was pretty sure. I had watched it during my ten minutes of espresso sipping. So I tipped my hat, paid the barista and walked down the street. It was crowded, but in an anonymous way. Tourists eyeballed everything. Vendors loaded with weavings and carvings eyed the tourists. Townspeople moved briskly eyeing nothing, probably heading back to work after comida. Everyone stepped around the blobs of rubber melted into the stone roadway, the remains of the gas truck tire that burnt the day before.

The sheet metal patches on the building were just lying propped up, sort of like the lean-to at Tío Rodrigo's chicken place. I did a quick look around, pulled the metal aside, and went in. It was dark inside, but sunlight slatted down through the cracks.

It smelled a mix of burnt dough, burnt coffee, and burnt wood. No burnt people. The floor had dried after the hosing it got from the firemen. Oaxaca was a desert, after all, but the floor was slimy and dusty to walk on. I would need another shoeshine. Pastry trays lay around, warped, scattered across the floor. There was no gas hose here. No cut-in-half smoking gun. I did not expect one.

The cracked concrete stairs gave a little when I climbed, but they held. The roof was still there. It tilted. A crack ran all the way across. I walked over to the rooftop propane tank, skirting the crack. The tank was still there too, sitting like nothing happened. And the metal fitting for the hose, the one that was filling up the roof tank when it happened, the one that was hooked to the truck below, was still screwed on. It had been hooked to the hose that had hung down over the side to the truck. There was no hose now. Just melted rubber. Nothing up here was broken. Nothing had come loose. I shook the roof tank. It was solid. And still warm. But maybe that was the sun.

The hose could have leaked a little, but not enough for a bomb, like what happened that day. I believed Efraím. It was slashed. I always believed him, but I believed him more after looking at the roof. I was mad again, too. My donuts were gone. My bakery was dead and in heaven.

I would work with Efraím. I guess I never doubted it. I wanted to be a don't-give-a-damn expat, the normal kind, but I had crossed some kind of line. Maybe I couldn't scare anyone, but I could try. I could sure scare myself sometimes.

First I had to go see about baby Jesus. The second posada would start soon.

As I turned back toward the stairs, a loud, different-sounding engine started. Not the rumble of traffic, or even the screaming of dirt bikes doing city duty. It was more like the grinding of garbage trucks in low, low gears as they stopped every other morning by my apartment. Then a metallic pumping and chugging of something hydraulic. Like the garbage truck was crushing every trash can on the block.

I walked to the edge of the roof and looked down. A bulldozer had pulled off a trailer in front. I had never seen one in Oaxaca before. Maybe never in this part of Mexico. If something needed to be leveled, a hundred men with hammers and shovels came to knock it down.

I would not have been more surprised if it were a flying saucer that I saw there. Mexicans do things in a small way. The bulldozer was big. Too big for Oaxaca.

Its treads were turning and one spun the bulldozer so that the thing came at the bakery, towards the wall I was on. Its scraper was aimed at me. It was picking up speed. It was going to hit.

No one knocks down a building in Oaxaca. They repair it. Buildings get propped up one more time. Churches get one more buttress. Old walls get concrete columns to brace them. Adobe walls starting to dissolve get new stucco. Even the termite-eaten wood–the finishing touch that everyone wants in order to make their building look colonial–stays as it is until only powder remains.

The bulldozer rammed a concrete beam. The roof's cement floor shook. Not quite an earthquake shake. It just jiggled a while, like a two story concrete marimba being played by a battering ram. I ran for the steps. I knew I could get out the side door so I turned at the bottom of the stairs. I got there just at the thing hit again. A beam over me cracked. Rebar held it together but it bent slowly and stooped like some old man, coming down and down toward me, like it wanted to whisper a secret. Then a chunk of concrete dangled under the rest and broke off over my head.

I thought, "Jesus, am I going to be late for your posada tonight."

****

It was red. And throbbing. A slow beat, four-four. Half way between a monster hangover and a hot iron hat, ten sizes too small.

I looked around. It was green. Light green on the top and half a shade darker below. The wall throbbed. The window pulsed a street view. A truck idled, keeping time with my head, on all cylinders.

A face came in front, a nurse, one who gave everyone injections for five pesos. She smiled. She held up a needle.

"*¿Cómo está?*"

Nothing came out. I shut my eyes, felt the jab. That was it.

I tried again in an hour, or maybe a day. A boy was there, this time a grandson of the Señora. He started yelling, the sound squeezed tight on my head and a nurse came in

"*¿Cómo está?*" Same question. The same one I got in my first Spanish class, the class I took in college and the same one I took again when I retired. I was ready. "*Bien.*" One word came out. It hurt to move my lips. I reached for the top of my head. My left arm and hand were locked up in a cast. I tried the other side and it still worked. I reached up and found a lot of cloth up over my ears.

"You were hit when the beam fell. What is your name?" It was a nurse speaking Spanish, just like everyone here does, but it sounded foreign. "I am the one that is foreign, like the bulldozer," that was what I was thinking.

"*¿Cómo se llama?*" she asked again.

"Santo Gordo," popped out before I could think hard.

"She bent closer and spoke softly. "Your real name, *por favor, y su fecha de nacimiento.*" My brain was hearing something. She was speaking Spanish, but I was hearing a mixture. Something soothing, a little scary. The tone was soft. The words were well formed, the way you would speak to your grandmother just before she croaked.

"Robert Evans, *dura cabeza a su servico.*" I got out a full string of words, a smartass one. Americans are always trying to be smartasses. I was not too smart that day after the bump. Maybe my whole head was a bump.

I gave her my birth date next. I got it right and passed the test. They were going to let me live.

"Now rest. You have visitors coming later, and you will need strength."

She smiled a nursey kind of smile and went out the door. The boy, Domingo–that was his name–stayed in the chair. He was the grandson always riding his bike in the courtyard. He was the one who ran errands for the Señora. He was the one she sent. The Señora must have given the order, "Watch Señor Roberto." That was me.

I looked around the room as best I could, lying flat and trying not to turn my head much. The room was big. Another bed was set on the side. This was Mexico and there was always a place for someone from the family to stay and take care of you and spend the night. Even in a hospital. That was where I was. A lunch sat on the table. Domingo was looking at it. I had my IV for a snack. It was all I wanted that day.

I could talk pretty well–to myself. If I did not move my lips, then my thoughts just jogged along. "Well, *Señor detectivo*, you certainly did it to yourself this time." I sounded like a Laurel and Hardy soundtrack talking to myself. I could not stop myself. "Big whack on the head. Phil Marlowe could not have gotten one better. But Marlow would throw back the covers and track down someone, maybe a killer, maybe a donut bomber. You are not made of such stuff, Señor Gordo." I was not listening to myself anymore.

Domingo closed the door. I was sure he was still there. He just wanted it quiet for me.

I was in a hospital. I looked around again—a big room, opening on a courtyard, a shower, a bed for the family, lots of fresh air, and cars. I could hear the honking in the road. It looked like an old hacienda, not a gringo hospital, no recirculated, ultraviolet air, no locked windows, maybe some shiny metal carts, but no curtained partitions anywhere. I was sure. Maybe stone arches, maybe a terrace, maybe a station with too many nurses according to any American staffing chart.

My head buzzed up an old memory. I was staying at my aunt's when I was sick that summer in New Jersey. That time when her family looked in every few minutes and worried about my measles. I got stuck there for two weeks and could not go home. They treated me like their own kid—I was almost. Everyone who had already had the measles came in to see me and when I got better, they played monopoly but with the lights down low. I think the same will happen here. My Oaxaca family will come. Except no monopoly. I will just ask them to read to me.

Something detective. And I will heal like I did back then. But with no play money. Only hospital bills.

The lights were low. A curtain was pulled across the window but sun was filtered in through its seams. The bathroom, off to the right, was bright. I looked away. Too bright for me. I had to go, but I had new plumbing. Plastic tubing leading over the side of the bed. That was fine. I could never get up that day.

The nurse put something in my IV. "It will help you rest." I got presleepy philosophical, thinking about life, thinking about burros going up and down the streets with loads of churros and wood carvings, and death, down in the ground and eating worms, and mezcal, here, deep in Mexico.

The IV drug explained everything to me. A near death, they call it, but it was nice to know things got simpler. I was not in Mexico because it was cheaper, like my friends had said, I was here because Oaxaca was alive. And I wanted to be, too.

Even the hospital was alive. The sick had enough family hanging around to have a fiesta. This was not a set of workrooms for hourly, not-quite-nurses getting minimum wage. Not a body warehouse. But a room with curtains and a breeze and a little boy who turned out the lights. And neighbors singing to their sick daughter down the hall.

I could see right through the walls now. The IV was humming along in my veins. The streets were alive. It was warm and bright. The Virgin Mary was coming in for a visit with her donkey and the street was full of people. The people, they had borne a lot. I could see the Spaniards, and hear the bullets chipping bricks in the revolutions and see landlords walking with their retinue of servants, like this was a falso-Europe of some Italian opera. The people here lived through it, somehow still decent and good to each other. In a clot of blood relations and family connections and neighborhood gatherings, taking care of each other. And somehow, it included me.

I got more greetings here in a block than I did in a week, back in the States. I knew every neighbor. We all went to the local posadas and weddings and funerals. We knew the cycle of each other's lives. Expats could join in–a little. We were given a pass, not as full family–everyone here knew gringos could fly off anytime–but as an auxiliary, one that participated and after years and years got to know some of the secrets of how the family was glued together.

I remembered back when I was a kid sitting on the Baltimore stoops, sweating and talking to neighbors, knowing the good guys and the bad ones walking by. My aunt explained all that. Girls hopscotched on the sidewalk. No one went inside if they could help it. It was too hot. And in the winter, everyone came inside, aunts, cousins, neighbors from down the street for Christmas and Easter. The city of my memories was alive like Oaxaca. But the city had died somewhere in the USA suburbs.

Maybe it still lived in streets of New York but for only a month in the spring when the windows were open, or maybe in North Beach in San Francisco for the dry part of the year, or for a couple of good days in New Orleans. Living in a neighborhood, living out a whole day in a couple of blocks. No air conditioning to lock you in. No closed windows to lock people out. Walking everywhere and getting food at the corner restaurant, with two tables and an aunt–not by blood but by hugs and *abrazos*. Her grandson was the *mesero*, the waiter, and she cooked and sometimes sat with you to talk about the flowers that would go on the altar this week and the new dress for the Virgin Mary.

Sometimes down here relatives were welcomed as big shots when they came to visit from the States, far-away big shots, maybe big in the landscaping, grass-cutting business. Or maybe selling Tupperware or ice cream.

Oaxaca and Baltimore, the Baltimore when I was wearing shorts at five years old, all got mixed together and finally, the room got sleepy, dead tired and black.

I woke. Time had passed again. It was dark. The dream went on, though. I watched the Americans down here, staying together, maybe too much, but active–a garden party, a book reading, a volunteer jaunt to build libraries in the *pueblitos*. Human engines chugging alongside Mexican life, Mexicans circled and paused and seemed to stay put. Americans traveled in straight lines, going where they wanted, but trying to go where the Mexicans went, never getting there.

I was back in the hospital. It was quiet. Only bugs looping around the light buzzed if they got too hot. Domingo was asleep on the chair. Mosquitoes had their feet planted on the ceiling. The night chill had them confused, forgetting why they came in the window, like me some days, walking into the kitchen and then, standing stock still, wondering why I was there.

The night was dead but the hospital was alive. It was like my aunt's back room, where I got well in '56. But this time with an oxygen valve stuck out the wall and a rolling IV stand made out of sheet metal, bent and welded together somewhere on the other side of town.

I was alive. I was a *Mexicanista*, connected to the Señora, my gringos, my friends. I was connected to the taxistas, maybe too much, and to the dead bakery and to my friend Efraím.

They needed me, the do-it-yourself detective. Or maybe, needed the gringo that knew el Norte and could rattle some heads up there, scare some folks. Well, this gringo would try.

In the States I was not needed by anyone, except maybe as a statistic to prove that boomers had boomed one time too many and finally exploded, deflated and were waiting around for a final goodbye. I read we were a statistic that took too much, a statistic that never knew how to give and now had nothing left. The hipsters taking over called us Social Security trash. I won't tell you what I called them.

Pain meds. They had my brain flying.

It was getting light—no, someone opened the curtains. The air smelled dry. My nose was an old leather tube. Or was there a rubber tube in there? No, that was yesterday. Today my nose was working and that was real air and perfume, perfumed soap, perfumed floor cleaner, perfumed nurse.

The door opened, Arturo and his wife Carmen came in. They had flowers. Carmen sat beside me. They were still. I peeked out and they saw my eyes open, now awake. We smiled.

"*Hola, Roberto, amigo mío.*"

I mouthed, "*hola.*"

Everyone sat still. Arturo was my first friend here in the city. I knew other people before him and sometimes even was invited to their houses, but Arturo had invited me into his family. I worked into his dream. I used to work water systems in the States. He did that for Oaxaca. Planning dams and aqueducts with water bubbling everywhere. I used sit around nights and plan with him. And drink a little.

But he had responsibilities now. He was in government. He was Catholic. He was a father with a daughter just about grown. And I was risky. I got my neck into too many things. He kept his neck clean. This must be Sunday. They were dressed up for church. Squeaky clean.

"Gracias for coming." I could talk. They nodded.

Then Arturo started, it was a sermon. "We want to help you, Roberto. You must learn to live here as a Mexican, not as a crazy American cowboy. You stand on the roof of an old building and stop progress. We will have progress. Money will come and things will change. You cannot keep it your Old Mexico playground, a playground for gringos. Oaxaca will not stay poor."

He had been reading the government newspaper too much. He never talked this way a year or two ago. Back when we hung out together.

"I have to tell you something. Your friend Efraím, I know he is a good man or wants to be one. He wants good, but he has gotten power suddenly, power that is not only

70

from money, it is from people who can hurt. They can hurt you too. You must be careful."

I nodded. Arturo was warning me. He had made his deal. Arturo would get something for his city water plan. He did not deal for himself. I do not know what he bargained away. His soul was at rest with the Catholic Church, so it was safe. He bargained away my bakery for a sewer line, or maybe a filtration plant? I think the bargain was for the new middle class Mexico. One with running water and parking lots.

"Arturo, I know you must tell me these things, and I thank you for doing so. Now go take good care of your wife and daughter. And work hard to make Oaxaca better. I understand."

I understood that life had gotten to him. He had to do this, warning me off from Efraím. For old times. Now he had to stay distant. It was part of life here when you had a position like he did, Assistant Director of Water Systems. Everyone owed as they moved up. And even if they moved up to do good, they had to sell a little of themselves, the part they did not save for family and God. Maybe you had to sell yourself anyplace you lived. I sure had. A couple of times.

I shut my eyes.

Sometime later I heard voices. Women's. They were not sure if they should enter. I called to them and they came in. It was María and Lupe.

They nodded and told me how everyone was praying. The Señora could not come today, but she sent them. They told me how they all prayed for me. I would recover. They knew it.

"*Su hija le llamó*"–your daughter called.

María handed me a note. I could not see without my glasses so I thanked them.

Spanish. The Señora wrote this in that neat handwriting they taught sixty years ago. I could see the tight loops but not tell what the letters were.

"Can you read it for me?"

María took the note and read slowly. Lupe looked over her shoulder. My brain made the translation.

"We told your daughter that you were hurt but would, with God's grace, recover. Your daughter Rhonda said she was coming. She will be here soon."

Then María and Lupe smiled. They said a quick prayer over me and left. I thanked them.

Rhonda–she told me she had become Randy–but maybe for the Señora she was still Rhonda. I did not know. But she would be coming to Mexico. That would complicate things.

I have not talked much about her. You must talk family all the time in Mexico. You live with them, you take the old ones out and carry the young ones everywhere. You ask about everyone else's. And you can hug any kid. You can kiss any baby even if you do not know the parents. Kids are Mexico. Families are Mexico. But for gringos, family is something you keep quiet. OK, some talk about children and grandchildren, but mostly to show pictures. No one talks about cousins and blood and marriage relations that spread out like some vine taking over your garden.

A lot of the Americans down here lost hold of their family. I lost mine. And now Randy was finding me.

Up north we have nuclear families. Mine had a nuclear explosion. My wife split, and my daughter Randy hated me for a long time. We did not speak for years. Randy and I had patched things up a bit. She helped me when I rescued Lupe last year.

I think Randy and I have gotten a little past those two modes of Gringos relationships–you love or you hate. Down here with a family big enough to populate small cities, you have all shades of feeling. Some you love, some you put up with, and some–there are always some–you hate, but you buffer them behind cousins and aunts. Or you just plain hide in the mass of people that show up for a party or a wedding or a death.

Randy was learning to put up with me. And I was doing the same. Not a bad relationship. Not great, but not horrible.

Randy and I were still working for Lupe. Randy was fighting in court in the States to get money from the father, the guy who kidnapped Lupe and raped her and got away with it because he was powerful and said it was consensual. She said he was the boss. This guy, the father was going to pay cash to get out of it. Randy was working with a lawyer for a good settlement. Maybe a lot. That was why she called. Maybe that is why she was coming.

They had handed me the note. I finished unfolding it. There was more on the back. I fumbled for my glasses and squinted in the darkened room. "Ronda explained to me that she will require your help on another matter. She will explain when she arrives."

I went back to sleep. I could not deal with too much at one time.

****

The next morning–I think that is what it was–Efraím was there.

"You sacrificed your head for the bakery. We will make little sugar skulls for you when you die. Ones with big cracks in them, like yours. We won't make them yet–you will heal–but will do it when your sainthood is complete and your bones are in a church down the street."

I looked puzzled. I was puzzled.

"Your scream stopped the bulldozer. Everyone thought you were dead and yelled. The woman selling jewelry in the street, the guy selling ice cream from his pushcart, the kids on skateboards, the tourists–they all yelled. When you stumbled out doing your blood-soaked zombie walk."

"The bakery walls are still there. The roof, no. But the bulldozer packed up and went back north when the police arrived. My lawyer came running that day and stood with the crowd in front of this historic landmark, Santo Gordo's Bakery."

"That is where we shall keep your bones when you die, better than a church. And everyone can view them when they buy donuts."

Efraím was trying to shake my hand. I was trying to sit up. I was not ready for my burial niche yet. I was pretty sure about that, even if the bump on my head was not.

Efraím talked fast Spanish. My head was going slow. He was sprinting, "I did not know that they would go this far to get the building. They would destroy it to steal it. Those Americanos would rather tear something down and rebuild than stay with something old. But you saved it. I am sure there will be donuts for you forever when it reopens."

I was having trouble seeing how that building would ever cook donuts again. But like the old Mexican Volkswagens that had been going from near-revolution times, or the bicycles and blenders always being repaired, or my patched up chair in La Avenida or everything else that never seemed to die around here, the building would go on, too. A little steel here, a little concrete there, a coat of stucco, and the pastelería would live again. Like me.

"You are better. The doctor told me." Efraím was about ready to do a big Mexican *abrazo* but the nurse came in and looked at Efraím like only nurses and schoolteachers can get away with.

"So everything is OK?" that was all I could think to ask.

"You are not OK." That was the nurse. "But I have some food for you. Time to give it a try. I understand that you used to like it."

I was worn out before I started, but it was food. I had my pride and forced eating. I had lucked out and smashed my noneating hand. The bad one just watched from the cast while his five-fingered friend righty did all the spoon work.

I mouthed the applesauce and drank the juice and then lay back. Efraím leaned down. "Nothing is OK, but that is all right. We are giving a fight. And do not worry about being in the bakery the morning before it exploded. When the two men were there. The government has declared it an accident, and the men you saw are gone. I will not say more. Goodnight, my friend."

I was not sure what gone meant. Maybe very gone.

Then he whispered "Oaxaca Chocolate. Remember that—the gringo company that wants the bakery. You will get them in the US. And I will stop their friends here."

My eyes were closed, the door closed quietly, the boy squeaked his chair as he pulled it near to watch over me, and the nurse stuck me in the rear.

****

Half of Oaxaca came by. They sat, they talked, they brought chocolate. They brought pastry. It was a perfect recovery.

The Señora came three times. The family traded duty to stand by and watch, but the little guy Domingo did most. He helped himself to the chocolates and pastries. I told him to. I had plenty.

Carlos came by and told me I better start writing the Santo Gordo book before they killed me. He had a buyer. Or someone who might be a buyer. Or something.

He was the start of the gringo procession. First came Willy, my neighbor, the one who kept a cheap room up the street from the Señora. He was an old socialist, blacklisted, I think, and then he retired and became a hippie. Then he retired again and came to Mexico fifteen years back. For him the revolution was still coming. He wore his union steward badge on his welders cap, even inside the hospital and everywhere else. He welded ships for thirty years until his lungs gave out. He said it was gas fumes but he had a lot of different fumes in him, for work and recreation. I liked Willy. He had a different slant from the guys who only wanted comfy in life. He wanted life to be hard. To him street blockades were salvation. He brought me a little plastic bottle of mezcal. That was how he made his life easy. And maybe a little dope now and then.

As he was leaving, a expat couple came in, Joe and Mary. For a while, they were José and María, like the holy pair with the donkey up on top of the Señora's dining room hutch, but after six months they gave up and went back to their Des Moines names. Joe and Mary fitted them. They looked more middle class than two SUV's in a three-car garage. They knew me from rooftop parties and the times when Joe tried to sell me a house in some new development outside the city. He always was almost getting into local real estate, but never quite. Mary brought me three novels, the kind that Oprah reviews. I put them in my maybe stack. Maybe they go to the library, or maybe I just leave them someplace.

Then Federico—the ex-Freddy, ex-car salesman, along with his girlfriend Luz—the ex-Lucy, and their neighbor

Linda, the retired art teacher. Linda was trying to make her name Spanish too, but found out is already was, in a gringo kind of way.

They brought me mysteries. I got to read about murders in Venice, deaths in Spain, and a great garroting in Paris. But that happened later when I got out. I was too busy to read in the hospital and the broken arm thing made reading hard, anyway. I had one good hand to hold the book spine; the other only had fingers sticking out of the cast to turn the pages—the cast came down to my knuckles. It worked but got me tired holding up that wad of plaster. But the thing was great for waving around to get some space on the way to the bathroom.

It was crowded in my room. I did not fight the visitors like my normal self and almost became social. I talked more than the Señora's parrot. But I kept my mouth shut when anyone asked why I was at the bakery that day it fell on me. Just hungry, I said.

It was nonstop. I held visitor hours every day in my room, and it was always full. Being a gringo in Mexico means you are nodding friends with any other gringo. You get invited to parties. Sort of like the rich used to do in the States. But here you just have to look white and speak English to get in. Money does not matter.

And you visit the hospital when something happens to someone that you hope never will happen to you. Visits are like a vaccination, a voodoo dance to keep away the Mexican evil eye, the eye that kills you in a car wreck, a lard-loaded heart attack, or maybe just from a bad case of hungry river amoebas gnawing on your liver.

But old gringos kept coming to Oaxaca. They ran away from the States and then clung together, looking for a little respite from Spanish and its fast, gun-shot syllables. Talking in slower English, they surprised themselves finding they shared much with other expats, stuff everyone thought was not important. Stuff no Oaxacan knew–old TV shows, movies, songs, Walter Cronkite, Rocky and Bullwinkle. Enough to make them comfortable. Even a socialist and a SUV suburban could hang out together, drinking beer and a little mezcal, and putting up with people they would never even meet in the States and even worse, liking them.

Gringos like to leave their mark on the world. I fought it at first, but then–what the hell. Everyone got to sign the cast. Just like back in high school. The Mexicans wondered at this American custom, not right for grown men, but they signed it too, shaking their heads at our primitive adolescent rituals. "Don't grow up," one of my crop of get-well cards said as it hung on a string stretched across the room. I had lost control. The nurses ruled my body and the visitors ran everything else.

Men told jokes, like usual, not caring if anyone paid attention, and women shared stories and feelings. It was like being caught together on a ship or maybe locked together in hell or heaven. Some place with pretty good internet and a Sam's Club and Walmart just outside of town and only a hundred or so people like you, to meet on the streets. Everyone else was different, no matter how good they were.

So they met in my room. It stayed full. And they brought wine and cheese and it was too much for me sometimes. I went to sleep and when I was lucky dreamed in Spanish.

I got my share of Oaxacan visitors too. Efraím poked his head in a time or two and said things were coming along. My neighbors came by and could never believe I was getting enough food. They brought more. A cook from the dead donut bakery came by with a dozen.

Someone always brought comida to a sick relative in Oaxaca. That was the way here. No one should be alone. If they had no family, they joined the damned and the hungry, because there was no food in the hospitals for the poor. Someone had to send it in. That was expected. Family was expected everywhere.

Oaxacan visitors were more formal than expats. They sat politely on their chairs and asked polite questions. I was polite back to them. It was nice but not comfy, not like with the gringos, giving me a hard time about my hard head. And my donut stash under the bed.

Of course now with Sponge Bob and Bart Simpson, Facebook, Justin B. and even Barney filling Oaxaca kids' heads with the same trash as the kids up north, I guess the politeness wall will break down after these kids age and eventually go to pasture and retire someplace. Everyone, Oaxacan and gringo, can be comfy together and half-ignorant except for TV cartoon and internet memories. Maybe world peace will happen when they tell stories about some hot Korean K-poppers in the big world meet-up in 2060 or so.

A couple of volunteers from the American Library showed up late one day bringing books. I asked for thrillers,

I asked for mysteries, but got chicken soup soul books and life improvement guides, all stuffed with happy-truths. One full of smiling puppy sayings reminded me to "Live like somebody left the gate open," and "If you make a puddle, don't step in it." That was where western philosophy was heading. Maybe religion too.

Those books got me well. I couldn't take any more of it. I had to escape. When the visitors left, I tried to think about life and afterlife but those puppy-brained books proved to me that all meaningful existence was dead. "Live like a dog." That was what I learned from them. Dogs do OK. They do not bump their heads.

One visit I did not have worried me. In fact, I did not hear more from Randy. She knew what had happened and I guessed she was in close contact with Lupe. But I was a little spooked just waiting and wondering what she needed from me. She would show soon, and then we would figure it out. She made a point of not needing me much, and I knew she could handle things, probably better than I could. Maybe that was why I was spooked. Why would she want help from me?

Noche Buena

I had done my time. The doc said, "Take it easy, watch the bad arm, do not scratch inside the cast, and go home." I was ready. My head was, too.

In the States a hospital gives you walking papers the first minute they think you won't die in the doorway. You get classes in nursing, the kind they should do–draining holes they left in you, cleaning up things dripping out of you. But they do not come by to visit. Only the bill collectors check on you, and if you are dead, they swarm to get their share of the remains.

In Mexico, hospitals keep you until you want to leave, until you go crazy if you have to stay another day. I could not take it anymore with the green walls and new flowers coming every day, but mostly with the visitors. I had gotten my pass and was ready to bolt.

I cut a slit in a real shirt sleeve, not the hospital thing, slid in my cast, and taped up the slit, like some medical incision gone wrong. I wrapped more tape to cover the bad calligraphy on the cast and was ready. Except for pants. The old ones had the dry blood look. Domingo ran home and got me a new pair.

They said my bills were paid. Efraím did that. Seventy bucks a day for a hospital room and about the same for the doctor. Oxygen was free but I do not remember trying any. A pretty good sum for Oaxaca, a thousand bucks for a week in the hospital, about the same as getting an emergency room Band-Aid in the States.

I owed Efraím, but he owed me. I stopped the bulldozer; the bulldozer stopped me–that sounded even. But the bulldozer was still alive and kicking with no down time while I was half healed but getting ready to kick back– or at least bash something with those two pounds of plaster wrapping my arm.

A guy in a white coat guided me to the door and stuck me in a wheelchair. We rolled out into the corridor. The Señora was waiting with her walking stick and tapped along beside me as we wound down a long ramp from my floor to the center courtyard. Sparrows sitting around the fountain squawked greetings. My old breakfast crumbs were now fair game. They took off for the second floor.

"You will be in time for *Noche Buena.*" She did not want me to miss the Christmas Eve celebration. *"¡Qué milagro!"* The Señora beamed as she explained God's miracles to me once again.

83

The real miracle was my head could crack Mexican concrete. Years of practice bumping doorways all over Mexico had finally paid off.

During my hospital stay I had missed most of the pre-Christmas posadas. One every night had been going on. That was OK with me. The season was too long for us Americans. We like our holidays tightly packaged ending with a big bang. There would be a big bang that night. Rockets from seven PM until two. Along with a mass in every church, processions up and down the city, the final posada, and the *cena de Noche Buena*—the big diner, and a drink or two. I was going to give it my post-hospital all, especially the *cena*.

I was feeling pretty good, but needed to practice being alive again. Hospitals prepare you to die. Your body does not belong to you in there. Anyone can stick in a needle or a tube anywhere they want. Things an embalmer likes to do to you. People watch you flat on your back, the same pose you will have in that fancy casket. Some come up and pray. You do what you are told—like you are in basic training for angel duty or, maybe if you flunk out, for devil work.

I had escaped my room. The day was bright with light streaming in from above the open courtyard. It was a good day. I had my pants on, and my head did not hurt. Best of all, my hair was parted showing everyone the long, jagged scar. Just right for a chat with Mr. Oaxaca Chocolate when I found him up in the States. I would give him a scare he would not forget. I was the new me.

But the old me needed to pay attention to where I was being pushed. Mexican wheelchairs, designed for shorter

Oaxacans, were dangerous. My all-American feet stuck out looking innocently at the cement all around. I pulled my feet up but the driver still whacked me into a door and a passing cart. I was getting out the place, so I did not care.

The wheelchair driver, the Señora, and I passed the courtyard, half circled the fountain ringed with poinsettias, and then turned into the short hallway leading to the exit. I got tilted over the curb and stuffed in a cab. I felt like something *relleno*–something stuffed–hanging out the cab window and waving goodbye to the nurses in the stone hospital doorway, saying so long.

I was alive. Whoopee.

The Señora put me on the sofa in the big room by the main door when we got home. She gave me soup, the same soup she had been sending me in the hospital. The one I liked with a big chunk of avocado floating in it.

But I was not the main attraction in the room. I looked over to the table. Virgin Mary and José, the two I had gotten down from the dresser, were getting ready with a garland wrapped around them and a candle or two nearby. This was their big night. Baby Jesus would take over the next day.

I napped and then it was time for the show. I had decided to walk the posada even if I was damaged. I declared myself mostly healed to the Señora and joined in.

They prayed as usual. The ceramic Mary, José and donkey led the procession. The household along with visiting family, neighbors, and friends walked in step with the songs. I lagged behind, waving my sparkler. Half way around the block, a troupe of guitarists and singers, ones the Señora had hired for that night, wearing fancy capes and hats, joined us and added some male power singing–all on the same note, well most on the same note–belting away. Ten big guys sang, and one small one who played athletic tambourine, jumped up and kicked high over his head, tapping the tambourine with his shoe, looking like a jack-in-the-box that had popped.

These guys were one of the local *tunas*, drinking clubs that first showed up in Europe's Middle Ages when kings had them wear fancy clothes and sing for their supper. They changed the pace of the posada, singing the same old songs, but faster and louder. They looked ready to break down the door when we asked for a place so Virgin Mary could have a warm room and maybe a manger rolled in.

My favorite part was when the door to the house finally swung open and the people inside sang:

> Come on in, you guys.
> You can have this corner of my place.
> This house is poor but I give it to you
> With all my heart.

The song was my story, what had happened to me. I had done my posada in Oaxaca when I first came and was welcomed in.

I finished singing and sat down but the *tuna* kept going. Everyone but the singers did posada snacks–another marshmallow clown for me. Then, low and behold, baby Jesus emerged from the Señora's room, dressed to the nines, looking like some midget courtier from the eighteenth century. That was how they dressed baby Jesus dolls down here. No swaddling, no diapers. He wore silks and gold lace, was drenched in perfume, and looked like a midget King of Spain.

Next came baby rocking. The *madrina*, the pay-for-it-all godmother, walked up and took the baby from the Señora. She held it like the Virgin Mary—the one stuck in the plaster statue—would want to, and rocked him back and forth. The *tuna* sang its heart out. Someone shot off rockets, maybe a dozen—I lost count. And after a half an hour of our loud, full-lung chorus and another smoky round of sparklers, baby Jesus lay down in the *nacimiento*, the nativity scene, in the manger between the camels and shepherds. Then we sat down and snacked some more.

That meant the night had begun. The faithful went to mass. The feckless watched TV. The Simpsons Christmas special was on. I shut my eyes and only cracked them a little when Bart yelled *"¡Ay caramba!"*—what Bart said down here—and the rockets went off again. I was happy. The family was hugging everyone everywhere. The kids were running around, knowing a piñata was coming up. What a night.

I could not doze off. I watched. Soon mass was over and the piñata rose in the night sky in front of me. One of the *muchachos*, an older boy, stood on the roof and pulled a rope tied to the top of the piñata. When it lifted over everyone's head, he yanked it back and forth so it danced in front of the fountain. The Señora got out her stick, taller than most of the kids, and pulled a blindfold from her pocket.

Seven paper cones, one for each of the seven deadly sins, stuck out from the piñata's candy-filled belly. I forgot all their names, but I knew gluttony was the one on top, the one nobody ever broke it off. Lust dangled down at the bottom and was an easy target.

The show started with the youngest children. They did not wear blindfolds. They could barely pick up the stick, but they tried and sometimes made contact with the hanging piñata. No damage and lots of laughs from the older ones.

Soon middle-sized kids, maybe seven or eight years old, whacked away blindfolded. I moved behind the sofa to get away from the wilder ones running back and forth.

This piñata was no paper tiger. It was a solid clay pot that took a man-sized whack, one stronger than this group of kids could make. It would not be broken apart until the older teens had their chance. But sometimes one of the deadly sins, those points sticking out, got knocked off and candy spilled. The children always moved in close behind the kid swinging in case some sin dropped. When it happened they ran in, ahead of the adults trying to keep order, and fell on the ground, right under the kid flailing with the stick. He was still trying to give a final good whump, but usually came closer to the plump heads of the children on the ground than he ever did the piñata.

The *muchacho* on the roof shook the piñata hardest when the biggest kids, the teens, got their swings in. Finally after a few failed to hit anything, looking foolish, missing and swatting nothing but air, one scored a lucky thump, and crack! Little kids fell on the ground again, this time after a pile of hard candy, Snickers, and even a few of the marshmallow clowns. I watched.

Potsherds stuck into knees and sometimes elbows of kids grabbing and packing sweets into their uplifted tee shirts or anything else they could find. They did not care.

The young ones went off into corners like wild animals after the hunt to gorge themselves. Older ones traded like stockbrokers. Parents came out and gave advice. No one listened.

Most of the sins had fallen on the ground with the remains of the pot. Gluttony and some of its friends still looked down, watching us, hanging by a few strands of rope, waiting for the Christmas dinner to begin.

It was midnight. Tables were lined up in the courtyard. A rent-it company had come earlier and left chairs and tables and plates and utensils. Fifty people would be eating. Local relatives sat in family groups, the visiting ones from the north squeezed in. Some tourists invited by the family stayed with their fellow English-speakers, some sat where they would speak Spanish. I sat next to the Señora's nephew from LA.

I did not talk. I drank and ate. We started with *ponche*, a drink made from chopped fruit and boiled and with spices, an old family recipe.

I had chips and guacamole. I was not sure if this was a real Oaxacan appetizer–there was an avocado tree in the yard, so it seemed local. But the northerners like the visiting relatives and me were the ones who dipped it up.

I had mastered one-armed eating, easy with chips, but harder when the real stuff came. The secret was to eat food well done. I was in luck. Oaxacans made everything well done. Or goopy–that worked too, using a big spoon. I was as fast with one hand as I used to be with two. Just messier. And I could cheat and hold a fork stuck into the fingers of the plastered-up hand. No one was worried about me losing weight.

The main course came. The young ones, the cousins, along with Lupe and María of course, served. First, I got a perfect mound of white rice, Mount Ricemore I called it. It was my sponge for the sauce that would be next. This was *mole* night.

I had spoiled myself on *mole*. Until a few years ago, it had been the special occasion comida, the wedding and holiday meal. But now every restaurant featured a *mole* or two. The grocery stores sold it in jars. Neighborhood shops offered homemade *mole* in plastic bags. I ate it twice a week. My *mole* affair had gotten almost out of hand.

Mole is a sauce. There are many *moles, amarillo, verde,* pumpkin seed, almond, but all start with an assortment of chiles and spices, in proportions never varied, made from recipes repeated down from long dead aunts and great-grandmothers.

I tried the different types but always came home to my dark one, my *mole* negro, my one with chocolate.

To make this meal, four women, two family ones and Lupe and María, worked in shifts stirring the black Navidad *mole* with a wooden paddle nonstop for a day. It bubbled in a two-foot wide clay pot, a special pot formed with a narrowed, thickening at the top, a collar to keep in the heat from the charcoal burning underneath. The pot was big. It held enough for a hundred. The family could eat *mole* for days.

Lupe laid a chicken thigh on my plate. This was no factory chicken. It had lived and died just outside of the city in a friend's big yard. It lived a happy Mexican life, like mine, I was sure.

María spooned on the *mole* sauce. I ate. I did not speak. The sauce was complex with everything blended together to make my mouth go wild. I tried to eat slowly, dipping tortillas in the sauce and drawing out each bite. I did slow down on the second helping.

I lived for a half hour out in space, off in eating heaven, and then returned and noticed conversations around me. I came back from my world of *mole*.

The family knew me and appreciated my eating. Some people do not show pleasure. I drooled it if I was not careful. That was the way to keep the Señora, the one who was the leader of the cooks, happy. She was proud of her food and wanted you to acknowledge her, to show her how good it was. I did that, easy.

Shots of brandy were passed. We toasted the Señora a couple times. We toasted the upcoming year and baby Jesus. Someone toasted Bart Simpson. Six toasts and I knew it was time. I climbed the stairs. Domingo came running to help but I did it one-handed, swinging my cast up in a final goodbye and then found my bed.

"Good night, baby Jesus. Goodnight, everyone. Santo Gordo goes to rest."

****

The day started with a crying baby downstairs, not Jesus, who arrived last night, but Lupe's little one. This hallowed day, usually the longest sleep-in of the year, started early for me. I could not get back into my dreams, so I went out on my balcony to watch the sun climb over the wall across the street.

Nature's traffic always amazed me when human things were still. Cars did not disturb anyone that day. They were asleep along with their owners.

Honeybees hovered everywhere. Every flower had a buzzing bouquet suspended over its petals and then bumblebees, two inches long, bombed their way in, or sometimes got lost and looked like an angry rock flying straight at me. They always veered off just in time to find a geranium or the big pink flower tree—some old-timer told me it was called a shaving brush tree because of its fuzzy-ended flowers, five inches long. I never tried it. I had a beard. But kids played with the flowers, collecting them, making dolls, teaching them to fly.

Sparrows cheeped in. Then, up high, pigeons did warm-up loops around the church. A Mexican blackbird, looking like a crow with wing extenders—he needed them because the air was so thin here—sat on the topmost point of a cedar, stretching like he signed up for a morning yoga class.

Then even higher than the pigeons, I saw two black-bodied, red-faced, hawklike birds with two white circular wing patches that seemed meant to scare small animals into

92

a fearful rigidity. They flew over, one with a lizard dangling from its beak.

Not quite the Aztecs' eagle with a rattlesnake hanging down, pointing to the promised land, the land the Aztecs promptly took over. This was a gentler signal to me, one that still had a little dangling death in it, but one showing that I too had found my place in Mexico. Montezuma, Cortez, and Jesus were here. I was too.

I looked over at my favorite ancient wall across the street. The sign "*Peligro*-Danger" had fallen off. More stucco had dropped, and the adobe was cracked from top to bottom. Bougainvillea were covering most of it, but it was ready to collapse. No one cared. People just crossed themselves when they passed by. As they did when the earthquake alarm went off.

I picked up the *pan dulce*s María had left me, those morning pastries of Mexico, too greasy, too sweet, and just right, and then brewed coffee strong enough to kill the dead. I gulped my first cup quickly and downed two sweets. That slowed my sugar hunger and speeded up my head.

I was ready to work. I had wanted to do this since that day in the hospital when Efraím whispered "Oaxaca Chocolate." This was what the web was for, so I one-handed it. You do not need two hands when you cannot type with more than one finger, so it worked fine. The web had Oaxaca and it had chocolate, it even had Oaxaca and chocolate together, showing bars made in the Centro, but it did not have a company with that name. Oaxaca chocolate was still a thing to eat, not a business taking over my promised land.

I put the keyboard away and looked back out over the balcony, I sat, I sipped, I watched, until I saw a cab coming up the street, the first car of the morning. Christmas morning was the deadest day of the year. Better than New Year's. Everyone, even infants had been up for their *cena de Noche Buena* to welcome the baby Jesus until 2 or 3 AM. And most were not going to get up even if baby Jesus needed changing.

The taxi stopped outside. I looked down and Efraím got out and came to the door. I waved and scared him. I was the last body he expected to see at this hour. I waved again and mouthed, *"Cinco minutos."*

I was there in three but half unbuttoned. Coffee sped me up but did not help with the buttons when I had a cast on my arm. I jumped in the cab and looked at Efraím. He was one of those guys who never seemed to sleep. I was one of the guys who tried to make up for it. I yawned.

"Good morning to you, too," he said turning towards me as we pulled out.

"Feliz Navidad." I gave him the greeting I should have started with.

"I want you to meet someone," Efraím was being his normal secretive self. He said no more about it.

"And, of course, *Feliz Navidad,*" he replied. Then he skipped the rest of the politeness he would have to do if I were a Mexican. Something was up.

We went to a house up in the *Reforma*, a small district about a mile north of my place, across the main boulevard, running north-south. They used to call it the Pan-American Highway back when Uncle Sam funded it in the '50's. He wanted smooth concrete to run from the US border to South America making it easy for army trucks and maybe tanks to chase down commies or anyone else he wanted.

Now it had reverted to its old name *Niños Héroes*, to celebrate the young military school cadets from Mexico City, heroes who wrapped themselves in flags back last century and jumped to their deaths from the top of the city's castle fortress, those fabled halls of Montezuma, rather than surrender to the invading Yankees. These cadet heroes were not battling heroes like our John Wayne, but ones who kept reminding Mexicans about their history. And how bad history can be.

The *Reforma* was a middle-class neighborhood. The stores were for Mexicans and not tourists. The restaurants, too, but tourists were infiltrating even here, across *Niños Héroes* and buying houses.

This was the time for globalizing. I was certainly doing it Well, at least I was western-hemisphering it.

We ended up in front of a modest one-story purple house. A low fence circled it—no tall walls edged the sidewalk here like in the Centro. A pair of yapping dogs welcomed us, bouncing on a lawn of true green grass, something you saw now and then up in this part of town now that Oaxacans watched American sitcom suburb TV and could buy water from the tanker trucks going by.

A man, maybe my age who looked like Efraím with his broad cheekbones and the nose hawking forward, came out the door. He matched me with his arm in a sling, bandaged from the wrist up halfway to the shoulder. Mine had a cast but no bandages. He won.

"This is my Tío Francisco." We did the intros. "He owns the bakery and I thought it would be best if he told you what happened before you see the Oaxaca Chocolate people."

We sat.

"They came three weeks ago. A Mexican, not Americanos. He offered me money for the building. A lot of it. I have had the building from my father. He bought it when he sold his land in the countryside. And he changed from corn and cows to pastries."

Efraím aimed Francisco back to the more recent past, "Who was this man who made the offer?"

"He looked like he was from Mexico City or maybe up north. He probably flew down on the early morning jet, I think. He was not here to enjoy Oaxaca. He is one of the new ones, coming in and trying to take over."

"He offered me a good amount, more than I expected. I do not know why. I thought he was crazy. Then he said he would be back. He was back the next day and raised the offer. I said it was my father's decision. He asked for him. I said my father died ten years ago."

"Then the inspectors started coming in and finding problems. Then the police. I knew the man with money had friends so I called Efraím. He called his friends and the newspaper wrote a story about how historical this building and its bakers were. How they baked the bread for the army in the '20s. Who knows if that was true? And things grew quiet."

Francisco sat still for a few moments as though he wanted to get the next part of the story exact. "Then the morning came. You were there. I saw you. Two young men I did not know, looking like thugs not businessmen came in and warned me to make a bargain while I still could. Then one pulled out a knife, a long one and made a slash near me. He laughed and made another and swung around and cut the hose hanging by the door. Gas came. I yelled and ran to the bakers in the back and ran to the sales people in the front. We ran across the street. Then I looked back and the glass exploded. They took me to the hospital, but first I called Efraím."

"So now you know." Efraím looked at me. "This is my uncle. They did this to him. But now I am watching for him. No one shall harm him."

Efraím meant next time.

Maybe something had already happened to those spikehairs and the other guy. Efraím never told me everything.

"We will go soon to the chocolate *fábrica* down past the Zócalo. That is where the Oaxaca Chocolate guy is, the American. He is working there. We will give him a visit. You and I will have a talk with him."

****

A day passed. No one did anything that week, the one between Navidad and Año Nuevo. Everyone lay around or touristed. The visitors from the States, both the ones with families who lived here and the ones just hiding from the cold and maybe from their own gringo relatives too, were on the streets every evening, parading up and down in the pedestrian-only areas, shopping and buying here and there. Street vendors were out in force. They all carried more than normal, more shawls, more blouses, more tree bark paintings, even more chili-cooked grasshoppers. The place was hopping. And tour buses clogged the city after driving down from Mexico City, filled with the sophisticated city folk out for a week-long holiday to discover their ancient Mexican roots, sort of like us Americans visiting old time, backwoods towns to absorb our history. Usually we faked it. We had plowed over most of our land's ancient cultures or put them in trailers on reservations. Not much tourist value there.

You could tell the Mexico City men, the *Chilangos*, on tour. They spent more on their clothes than the Oaxacans. But the middle class and upscale women, both Oaxacan and *Chilangas*, dressed classy and wore heels so high it was hard to tell them apart. Indigenous women wore homemade sandals and their own homemade clothes. You always recognized them.

I lay around that week. Healing I called it, eating hot meals from the Señora and getting in some good street watching from my balcony. I had taught Lupe how to make iced tea and they brewed it for me, even though they hated the stuff. They kept trying to sneak in herbs and other plants they said were good for me. As long as they sugared it up, it was ok. Probably plain water with enough sugar would be ok.

Getting almost bumped off moved me up a notch on the saint ladder. I was enjoying my new stepped-up view on saintly life, one where I did not ask for much, only a couple more tomorrows and good food today. But I knew I would be dropping back down to earth soon, when we went to see the American in the chocolate shop. Then I would be praying for a lot more than food.

Efraím would be coming for me. I was ready to get back on the case. The doctor had not sent over any more pills, the bandages were gone and my headaches were mostly a bad dream. Only my arm in its plaster cast reminded me of the concrete coming down. I was almost my normal decrepit old self.

Efraím came on the Tuesday after Christmas.

"Time for us to go. He is in the local chocolate store right now."

We charged out the door past a group of young American men down for Christmas, doing missionary duty, wearing cheap suits, plastic nametags, and carrying pamphlets. The holidays brought them. They started after Efraím. He crossed himself as though a vampire had flown at him. I jumped in the cab. The missionary boy saw I was only a fellow countryman and took off. We left them in the dust. No good works for you guys today.

We passed through the tourist area and went into the working part of town, driving by the businesses that had real things—welding shops, paint stores, sheetrock suppliers, plumbers, all closed and waiting out the week, waiting until after New Year's to reopen. Shops for everyday people, however, were open—clothes, shoes, jewelry, and, of course, the pawnshops hoping for your old gold. Some with big inflatable signs. Some with men in costume waving posters. All with guards and fat gun belts. Everyone needed money these days. Even thieves and pickpockets. They were around, too.

We inched closer to the old market where the traffic was stopped. Stalls blocked half the street to sell Navidad specials–sunglasses with any logo you wanted, ditto for purses. CDs and videos with home-printed labels hanging from metal racks, next to the latest, just-copied computer games and software. Curly potatoes and bananas were deep-fried in front of you. Piles of chili-covered grasshoppers spilled over from woven baskets. Kids, five or six years old, wandered about selling chewing gum that they carried in a little wooden box hanging around their necks. Old men grabbed your sleeve as you passed and showed off hand-carved walking sticks with lion-head handles. I was glad we were driving, you could barely walk on the sidewalk–there was no room.

Efraím backed up with a high-speed parking maneuver and ended up in front of a lime green two-story building proclaiming "Santa Juana Chocolate and *Mole*. Founded 1930." The stucco was recently painted, but you did not notice it, you stared at the wood trim. It glowed like my shoes after the shoeshine guy laid on five or six layers of wax. The wood trim was a bright, clear pine covered with layers of lacquer, making it shine like God was hiding inside. The wood panels outside glowed in the sun. Everything wood inside reflected light. Desks, counters, and shelves stood out from the white-washed walls. I had not seen anything like this down here before. Everything was normally stucco or stone and painted in colors not found in the States–parrot green, grape purple, flamingo pink. But wood, you never saw it. Wood was created by God to rot and be eaten by termites, not to hold up buildings.

We went inside. To the left was the demo area, to the right the showroom lined with chocolate boxes in different colored wrappers–green for bitter with almonds; brown for coffee-flavored; red with orange peel; and blue, the one I wanted, laced with honey and chile.

By the door, stone bowls filled with different *mole* sauces spilled out complex chile-chocolate smells, calling on me to sample. They were next to the *crema de mezcals*–coffee, banana, and about any fruit you wanted, along with twenty percent alcohol. A man in a skinny tie, the cashier, sat in a wooden booth. It shined like everything else. A group of European tourists stood surrounding the cashier, waving chocolate boxes and money.

On the other side, the demo area, seven big metal grinders whirled. Three Oaxacan men loaded them. Another young man in the company's uniform shirt stood by, looking very 21st century Californian in cargo shorts, blonde hair, and flip flops.

The metal grinders looked nineteenth century. Man-sized electric motors turned everything. They had replaced the burros when electricity came into this neighborhood. The motors drove leather belts turning rough millstones hidden inside the grinders' casings. Each grinder stood five feet tall, anchored in a line along the wall. Old dented sheet metal covered their gears and pulleys. Some long-dead manufacturing company's logo was embossed on the top. Each grinder had chutes leading into the top, filled with cocoa beans, vanilla sticks, and almonds. Another chute stuck out from the bottom, dripping chocolate paste.

The California-looking kid was handing out tiny spoons so we could try the paste. I tried—bitter as medicine.

The top chute emptied as cocoa beans were pulled in towards the grinding stone. A screw turning in the top chute pulled the mixture in. The screw was six inches wide, two feet long, and spinning fast enough to grab your hand, shake it, and twist it into braids. The three men loading beans moved fast, pushing with a stick, scraping the edges and when something was stuck, poking in fingers and pulling them out fast. All ten.

I walked up to the American. He was our guy.

"You got a gig here?" I tried to talk Californian. I was friendly, like a tourist, but thinking like a detective. Efraím stayed in the back of the crowd.

"Sort of, on vacation from college in San Francisco and checking out chocolate companies. I tried to get into the other one. The big one. But I got in here for a couple days. Nice people."

"You make chocolate?"

"Mostly I answer questions in English. They are afraid I will get my fingers caught, like they say the new guys always do. And I am only here another week. Classes start."

He was leaning back on the cashier booth. He offered a spoon to my good hand. I took it and tried again. Sweet this time. Almost sugar. This was not the chocolate I knew, but it was one Mexicans loved.

He held the plastic spoons out to a new group of Germans who had just entered. They acted like he might give them a disease and turned away.

"So this is for a class?"

"Sort of, I am taking pictures and doing a power point slide show, but also I am showing everything to my uncle, the chocolate man. Tomorrow I am taking a cooking class, all in the interests of chocolate."

He was your basic up-north guy, like me, ready to talk his head off to anyone. But I was getting somewhere. There was a chocolate uncle involved.

"He's going to make chocolate in the States. And be the Starbucks of chocolate. I'm not joking, but I'm not supposed to tell anyone about the Starbucks thing."

"Does it taste good?" A woman with a Russian accent had figured out that the American was part of the chocolate demo and reached for a plastic spoon. She cut in front of me.

I went out on the street and talked to Efraím. "This kid is clueless. He got a paid for vacation by his uncle who is the boss of a chocolate company. Oaxaca Chocolate, I bet. To take pictures. Can you get someone to follow him, maybe check the people he telephones? Where he lives?"

"Already did. He calls his girlfriend a lot in the States and another one down here too. His name is Andy Rathman. He lives in a place called Pacific Heights near San Francisco."

"Whew, that's a money area. You needed a group marriage hooking up two or three doctors and a rich lawyer or two to afford a place in that neighborhood."

Pacific Heights was the rich heart of San Francisco, clogged with money, a multi-million-dollar-plus area–and that was for a flat, not a house.

This family had enough money to dangle some down into Oaxaca.

Efraím and I went back in and sat in the little restaurant at the back of the store. I ordered a hot chocolate drink with chile, Efraím ordered one with orange. It took a while. We watched as the waitress did the wooden spindle trick, frothing it up in a bowl that Montezuma might have used. The bowl was cracked enough.

Mostly we watched the gringo kid up front. He did not do much. He was on the phone, with a girlfriend. You could tell by his voice, cell-phone loud. This local girl was not waiting much longer for him. He hung up and went to the boss. The boss looked like he had had enough for a while and the kid left. Maybe he was fired. I could not tell.

"This kid is nothing. You need to go up north and see the uncle, who has the money and blew up Tío Francisco's bakery." Efraím said it like a judge up on the bench or maybe like a general lining up his troops.

This uncle's chocolate business did not make any sense to me. Why would he buy a shop in Oaxaca when he was making chocolate in the States. No one would steal the methods here, hundred-year old grinders, chopped-off fingers, chocolate too bitter or too sweet for most Americans.

I had read about the fancy, all-American, artisanal movement–little breweries, little bakeries, and now little chocolatiers, but this uncle sounded big, not little. For big, you do artisan PR, but you cook with trainloads of ingredients, industrial-grade stainless steel, and push-buttons. Not Oaxaca's artisan way with sweat and a hundred Mexicans working fourteen hours a day.

A cab driver had picked up our Mr. Rathman. We did not hurry. We knew where he was going after the taxista called us with a report. A nice hotel, the Oaxaca Royal. More money. This kid was not slumming. His hotel advertised itself full of food, flavors, and flowers and had a cooking school for up-north foodies.

It was time for me to try a cooking class and learn more from this Andy kid. I might even learn some cooking and get past homemade ham sandwiches, guacamole and beans, my food triangle, the one I used when I missed my restaurants' hours and the Señora was gone.

****

I signed up and went the next morning. Andy was there, in front. He was taking notes. Others were too. This was a religious service for foodies.

The class slid around in their seats, juiced up, waiting to watch the famous local chef, Señora Álvarez. I was jumpy too, but not from any chef groupie thrill. I wanted to eat.

The class description said breakfast included, and I was hungry.

I was the ancient one, looking even older than usual with my new scalp scar, my arm in a cast, my grey beard and my old-leather skin. I tried to fake some youthful enthusiasm, studying the chocolate paste in front of us, thinking about dipping in a finger and giving it a taste, but I did not want to stick out too much so I just looked.

At nine AM we were called to order at a long table in a kitchen bigger than my whole apartment, singing Mexican songs and drinking–you guessed it–chocolate. Our lesson in *molinillo* spindle technique, mixing and frothing, made a great, good-tasting mess. Then we had egg-yolk bread to dunk. No donuts, no churros, but this rich bread dunked fine.

Señora Álvarez explained that you do not add any milk to real hot chocolate–I knew that. We were going to be authentic that day. Authentic was the word said most often by our teacher. Everything we would touch grew or walked on local native nearby dirt. My classmates were in heaven.

Señora Ávarez's involvement with food was more than cooking. She had obviously partaken often of her work's end result and grown into a bouncy, plump, rounded type. She kept us in a bouncy mood. I don't usually do that. I don't bounce. I eat and flop.

But for this day, even though I hated to admit it, this was kind of fun, like being back in kindergarten, doing song time and getting our morning hot drinky.

The class of nine Americans buzzed. They were one-weekers, still excited that they were wearing shorts and sandals early in the morning in December, not snow boots and insulated everything. They kept joking about sweating this early in the day. Sweat was good after you leave ice-slippery roads and snowed-in airports. Sweat was great for a week or two.

These guys were excited about food. They talked tastes and compared chocolate to burnt umber tones and some other words normal people never hear. Or maybe these younger foodies were the new normal. They kept talking about food art. I kept talking about "when will we eat?" I don't mind the art part—you can talk food all you want, just do not replace food completely with words—that's when I go crazy.

We headed out as a safari into the depths of the market, not the big one run by the Oaxaca mafia, but the smaller one, probably run by them too, that caters to city people and tourists. It covers two square blocks down by the Zócalo and has hundreds of stalls. We went to the meat section. You name it and that body part was lined up waiting. Then down to vegetables, spices and herbs. Señora Álvarez wanted us all to bounce with her through each stall, sampling, smelling, remembering, describing tastes. The class ate this up. They took pictures and posted them on Facebook, Twitter, and every other site that allowed you to trumpet your conquests, food or otherwise.

I tried to get up near Andy, but he was still in that first flush of fooding. The front row was going gaga over the goat neatly laid out in a butcher's stall. It looked like the dissection class I had done in a biology course a long time ago. I hung in the back and figured I could talk better to Andy when we got back and were cooking.

Thank God we reached the chosen breakfast stand. Señora Álvarez had picked a good one. I got my eggs, barely out of the chicken, cooked just right and made into that paradox in this Catholic country, divorced eggs—one egg in green sauce and the other in red, both on tortillas, with a line of judicial beans keeping the two spouse-eggs separate.

People could not get divorced here. Eggs could. You kept your rotten husband forever in Oaxaca. You split with an egg just because he bathed in a different sauce. But the Pope did not care about chickens, so it was ok.

I was lucky. Divorced eggs were two breakfasts in one. One green and tangy, the other red and spicy. And the refried peacekeeping beans were a bonus.

"Sauces are the secret of Oaxaca. Food is only a canvas underneath for the art of sauces to paint upon." The Señora was a Nobel professor to these guys. Her garbled words would be shared all over the web world. The class already shared about a hundred pictures and we had not started cooking.

I ended up sidling next to Andy when we got back and started the prep work. I was masa man, making the corn tortilla dough. Try that with one arm out of service some time. Andy was bean guy. He squashed. I mashed.

"Hey, you came in the chocolate place yesterday. I work there," Andy called to me between bean mashes.

Work was the wrong word to describe what Andy did in the chocolate store. The Mexicanos running the grinders for twelve hours a day were the ones working. Andy was doing easy time for his uncle.

"Yes, that was me. I am Roberto."

"*Me llamo* Andy." He had his Spanish intros down. All tourists learn that. And the handshakes and the *mucho gusto*s, too.

"I thought you were doing chocolate?" I was not chatting, I was detectiving.

"I am doing everything. I study at the Culinary College in San Francisco. I cook. That is why I am here. To learn the literature of food. That was what my advisor said."

"I thought you were doing chocolate?" I stuck on that line.

"Oh, that is for my uncle. He paid for this trip, so I have to put in some time. He is the boss up there, Oaxaca Chocolate, you know."

I was getting somewhere. He said the magic name. He also kept mashing beans into paste. The teacher came by and plopped in some lard. She smiled. Andy beamed. He had the student thing down. She looked at my one-armed masa. No smile. She took over and kneaded a while.

"Like that," she said and left. But she had two-armed it. I went back to my one-handed dough slapping.

There were no grades here, just smiles—that was what she promised—but no matter what, I would get to eat at the end, even if I flunked.

I kept pumping Andy. He kept pumping the beans. They definitely would not need much processing after you ate them. He raised his hand for the teacher, "I'm done," and went over to the more complicated part of the kitchen.

They were doing sauces. I kept going on the masa, thinking about wacking it a couple times with the cast.

My next job was making little round masa boats called *memalitas*. They would have floated fine. At least until I filled them with Andy's sinker bean goop and sprinkled fuzzy Mexican cheese on top. They were too heavy to float, but certified ready for the oven, so I was transferred to the *agua fresca* division. This was the normal job for five year olds on the farm, stuffing fruit in the water after cleaning their hands. I did better than most kids, especially on the hand-cleaning bit. At least on one hand. They had me put a plastic bag over the cast.

The students were mostly done and comparing stories and sharing Facebook names. One had a catering company, and the rest just had fancy tastes and vocabularies. I decided not to talk about my apartment microwave after they started comparing ten burner stovetops and imported multilayer pots and pans, whatever they could be for.

We finished. I got a little more out of Andy. He was one of The Rathmans. The food Rathmans, he explained. They were a big deal in San Francisco making some kind of oily chips, I think. But they had an uncle who was a Silicon Valley Rathman, one who lucked into a pile and wanted to move it into the hot new field of foodies, not the old family junk-food tradition. Wine was taken, coffee diluted, and bubble tea popped before it ever took off, so Mr. Money Rathman, the uncle, convinced himself chocolate was the future. He wanted to move his money from software to cocoa. I never did find out who his man in Oaxaca was. The one who was trying to buy the bakery. The one who paid to blow up the bakery. I was sure it was not Andy. He was a floater. I was looking for a shark.

We ate for three hours. My bean boats were a hit. Andy and I bonded over them. We exchanged e-mail addresses. And did a fancy upscale knuckle bump. You couldn't get much closer than that.

Class ended at four. I rolled out after coffee. Everyone's bounce was gone. Even Señora Álvarez sagged. I dragged home, right up to bed for a siesta.

****

"I'm here." Someone called up the stairs.

I was lying flat. It was dark. I napped all the way through my post lunch snack. I was still full from the class but it was wearing off.

She walked in. "It's me, Randy." She gave me a little kid kiss on the top of my head right by the scar. A daddy kiss. It was the first one in a long time. We had some hard times, Randy and I, but maybe times were a-changing, as she used to tell me. I would wait.

I got up, way too slow–I was still sleep-dopey–and one-arm hugged her. She patted the cast like it was some lost creature, then smiled and looked around my room, at my rugs and crazy animal woodcarvings, all the local stuff that moves in with you down in Oaxaca if you spend enough time. It all impressed her. The disorder impressed her too, I could tell, but she did not say anything. Then Lupe brought

111

up the baby. Randy broke into a smile, so big it looked like it hurt.

I was starting to think Randy had turned out OK. Like a nice car with all the extras after it got a few miles on it. She had grown up, not with much of my help. Sometimes you are lucky.

You can tell when they are finally grown. It takes a while, but they look different. Like they are in charge and you are on the sidelines. Not even the coach anymore, more like a ready-for-the-farm cheerleader.

She looked like me, but without my sagginess. She had a sharp eye—I had to call it that—tight bird eyes. They jumped from thing to thing. She did not gaze as I do. And she looked ready, like someone on a mission, not a stroll. She was not yet in full tourist mode, still Americano and wound up, right off the plane, looking the part too, with her work haircut framing her face, not fancy but definitely not cute and with her clothes neat, tidy, utilitarian but somehow snappy with everything lined up and color coordinated. She was pretty. But she did not push it over the edge. She had makeup—I could feel the lipstick smear where she did the kiss. And she had a tattoo, on her shoulder. An artful one, I would say, with a tree and a bird and intertwined flowers, not too big. Artful, that was not that hard to say. You have to change with the times.

"You guys, I bet you and Beto are pals." She was sparkling. I kept thinking someone had done a magic wand job on her to make her this happy.

I had to respond and did not want to bring her down. "Well, I watch him every once in a while." It was sort of true. I watched him from my balcony when he was down by the fountain.

She did monster hugs with Lupe. They had become sisters-plus when she and I did the rescue to bring Lupe back to Oaxaca. It looked like it was still in effect.

Baby Beto ended up in my lap when the women went downstairs. I guess it was time he and I got more acquainted. I figured it might happen more often now that Randy was here running off with mama Lupe. But it was OK, I was not doing much. Detectiving was not a full time job. And babies are better than dogs, they say, to cheer you. Especially, if you can hand them back after an hour or so.

Everyone said I needed cheering after the headbump. But really it was the explosion that got me down. That and thinking about what to do up in the States with Uncle Chocolate.

The cast helped with the baby. It had a bend at the elbow, and Beto fit right in. Like it was a cradle or a football carry.

We did not stay upstairs long. I was hungry, ready for cena. Baby Beto and I went down. My stomach was angry at being ignored. It growled like some nasty pet dog or maybe a wolf, but Randy still had to be introduced downstairs. My stomach was getting worried. I was afraid it would start snapping at everyone.

This was Mexico. When someone shows up, you have a half an hour or so of intros, sitting in the special living room, the one with chairs all covered in plastic used only for guests, with, at best, a cookie. We sat there with the Señora.

Randy was patient. She smiled. She was good with this sort of thing, then Lupe came in and took the baby from me. Randy did a double hug around the two of them, and then she took the baby. That ended all formalities. Randy was a baby kisser and Beto loved it. The room turned giggly, except for the Señora and me. We sat still. She held her knees together and I held my stomach.

As Randy bounced the baby up and down, I had my chance. I ran up the stairs mumbling an old-man bathroom excuse and dug out my reserve, hidden in a metal box, something military, far back under the bed. I told everyone it was for earthquakes, but I hit in times like this when Mexican courtesy delayed eating.

I sprung the catch. The Marias, the cookies that could live forever in their shiny cellophane wraps, waited for me, lined up ready for inspection. They said these were tea cookies, but I did not worry about the tea. They worked dry but were tough, and crumbled if you fought them. They were sweet, but just a little. Perfect for a filler. And to top it off I slathered on peanut butter. That made them undunkable, but nothing wet for a good dunk was around.

I had four or five and clogged up with throat gunk, but the cookies saved me and my stomach from complete emptiness as surely as those all-American missionaries a while back would have saved my empty soul, that is, if they had not run when they saw I was a devil-smiling gringo. Missionaries only saved born-here Oaxacans. We expats were on our own. Luckily I kept cookies around for my salvation.

I went down the stairs, and Randy came over and asked how I was. She rubbed a smear of peanut butter off my beard and gave a hug, one that felt pretty daughterlike. Something had happened. She thought I was a capitalist bandit ten years back. And she thought maybe I was a very junior drug lord when I explained two years ago how I lived in Mexico. Now she seemed to think I was dad.

"I am only here four days, so you have to be a tourist with me. You always said Oaxaca was a special place. Now you have to prove it." I could not argue with that, and my agenda was open, as always.

She went back to baby Beto, and I went back to my chair. I twiddled around while she talked with Lupe and the Señora. She was a talker–in Spanish, that is. I could understand most of it. It had to do with the upcoming settlement from baby Beto's father, the one who kidnapped Lupe. Randy and a lawyer from one of her nonprofits fought for her. They did not think going after the father in criminal court would do anything, so they went for his money. He wanted to fight, but his lawyer said settle. His wife said she wanted to strangle him. So it was getting settled.

I was starting to get proud. She had done well. Beto would do so too. And Lupe along with him, of course.

Then Randy stood up. "Hey, I am hungry. I haven't eaten since the airport in the States." She rubbed her stomach. Takes after her father.

This was my second chance of the evening. I was my Santo Gordo best, fixing up problems. I am best on food problems.

"Don't worry. We can get something right down the street." I did not want the Señora to have María cook anything. That would take too long. Good, but slow, that was the way in the house.

"Lupe and Beto must come too," Randy said. And they did, with Randy holding baby Beto like he was hers as we walked out the door. Lupe smiled and we walked off. The Señora stayed back, wondering what happened. That did not happen often, letting Lupe free. I had a feeling it would be happening more with Randy around.

We went three blocks over to the New Agey restaurant, lots of fruit and juice and natural veggie things. Ones that cost a lot. Not like the fruit and juice in normal restaurants that were cheaper and tasted the same. I had never been there before. Randy liked it. She was a veggie person, I was sure.

I had two *pollo* sandwiches. Sandwiches work with one hand. You do a rip and chew, no fork or knife needed.

These were the leafiest chickens I had seen in a long time, crawling with sprouts. Even worse, you could plant the buns—enough seeds to grow a garden. The bread was organic enough to mulch with. But they were edible. I am not complaining, well maybe I am. I could have used some tortillas and—health be damned—lard, shredded pork, and beans. With some green sauce. But not in that place. Only free-range mayonnaise was available.

I hadn't realized how much Oaxaca had changed from its classic tortilla days. It had become not only globalized but also updated into a new-earth version that included vegetables, ones I had never even seen back in the States.

116

Well, at least not until I was thirty-something and away from my family's potatoes and peas.

Randy ate a veggie wrap. Wraps had always been Mexican–they were called tortillas–but now in its new up-north name it came in a dark green color, one certified fat-free. And worst of all, not a bean in sight–a Mexican sin.

But everyone was doing fine. Lupe got a fruity drink. Baby Beto played with the straw. My stomach behaved.

We talked–baby chatter. Beto got passed to me so the women could talk better or maybe to have me talk less. I was eating one-handed pretty well so it worked fine.

Randy and Lupe slowed down and then stopped. They had run out of steam. Probably Randy was ready to crash after the flight. Who knows when her trip had started, probably yesterday midnight. That is when the Mexican airline specials like to leave.

Randy turned to me, "We definitely go touristing tomorrow. I am only here until New Year's, only a few days, and I do want to see this place, your city. And we can talk. Talk about the problem."

She meant her problem, not mine. Then she turned back to the wrap, chomping unladylike on the last green bite. She was an eater. She really did take after her dad.

We went back. Randy slept. The Señora had an extra room for her. I went to the balcony and watched the moon, wondering what I was getting into. Exploding bakeries were one thing, but a daughter with problems was a new world for me.

****

She woke me early. The birds were up. I never noticed that birds and trash trucks were the main things moving at 6:30. I had told Randy it gets too hot for me up in the ruins, the big ones at Monte Albán. My plan had been to just stay there a short time; hers was to go early and do half the day.

But first I wanted to go see the place that put me in the hospital. On the way there, I told Randy about the bakery—well, not everything. But enough to get her interested.

The cab driver was friendly, not an Efraím, but he liked talking. Randy peppered him with questions about family, children, where they went to school, all that stuff. I asked about the knock in his engine that sounded like it should have fallen apart a long time ago.

The ruins from the bakery were still pink but dirty. Two thirds of the place was standing. Police wrapped everything in crime scene tape. It looked like tape was holding the concrete columns from falling. There was not much else. Bricks were in a pile. The wood was burnt. The tape warned everyone, "Careful-*Cuidado*." Most people paid attention to that. I would, too, these days.

Six-foot sections of sheet metal were lying against the one wall that had fallen. I could have gone in again if I had wanted, but I was not stupid. I am one-time stupid. At least without a helmet and a good reason. My bum arm plastered in the cast along with my mostly-recovered head made me think twice, sometimes more.

Randy and I examined the street in the front of the bakery. No one in the press had explained how the building got knocked down on me. Some said it just fell, God willed it, but I had heard a bulldozer. I felt the thump when it hit. Now it seemed like a phantom that no one talked about.

But on the street tread tracks ran in front of the old donut window. Fifteen yards of marks drove straight toward the bakery–right up to the fallen wall where it did the bang and bump. Then the tracks backed up, and returned where they started. What a detective I was. Randy looked at them too. I had a witness.

I was lucky. Streets in Oaxaca are soft. Sometimes your shoes get stuck when it is hot. Perfect for bulldozer prints. I needed to talk this over with Efraím, soon.

Santo Gordo needed a detective kit, like the one I had as a kid to make plaster casts of footprints. Like they do in detective shows. Sort of like they did on my arm when it was broken.

Instead, I took a picture before everything melted back down into the street after the sun baked it for a week or two more. Someone did this to me. Broke my head and my arm. I wanted to know who.

"OK, Mr. Detective, we got your proof, now let's go see those old ruins." Randy did like ruins, the old kind that were in the hills. Not the bakery ruins.

I agreed with her. No more detecting. One more day waiting to talk to Efraím would not make a big difference.

We got back into the taxi. The early morning air had chilled us and then it got cold as we wound up the mountain a thousand feet or so, climbing above Oaxaca.

The sun was not hot–it would be soon–but it was bright when we got out of the cab. No clouds anywhere, like normal. I put on my tourist hat, the big one. I did not want the sun rays to bake me.

Most vendors had not set up yet, but the straw-hat guy probably slept there. Randy bought a big one and looked ready for the beach. I pulled mine down tight and looked like an old man, the kind that lie in the sun and don't move much. That was my goal for the day.

But first I did a little dad duty. I showed her the ball court in the ruins, my favorite part of the place. Its stone hoops had snakes carved around the thing. I did my guide talk about the solid rubber ball, the hoops, and the rules–no hands, like soccer but with raised baskets. Randy listened politely but looked at the cut rock walls and terraces.

Randy asked how long did take to make one? How many years did it take to build a court like this? They had no cement–the place was solid rock and there was nothing for carving it but other rocks. I just shook my head.

I knew more about the players. Teams played their hearts out when this place was running full blast a thousand years ago. Someone, probably a priest, cut their hearts out, postgame. Some said winners got the knife–God should get the best. Others claimed it was the losers who got it– otherwise they saw a motivation problem, but only one side lost their hearts and moved up to the elite eight or maybe higher in the human sacrifice chart. Sports were big religion back then, like now. Think World Cup soccer, the NBA, and Texas death row all combined into one.

We climbed the steps to get out of the ball court. "That's it. Time out," I said. "I'm going back to the café to hydrate. Doc's orders." She nodded like she expected that.

"You're barely out of the hospital, not some crazy twenty-something. You are old." I guess that cheered me, anyway I got to rest in the shade.

Before continuing her exploration Randy sat down beside me and started talking. It was serious. "Dad, last year I thought something crazy was going on down here with you, like maybe the cartel or something after your visit up north, but I checked on you. I did some research. You were one of the good guys. I never would have guessed."

I waited for her to explain more, but she did not. She turned and took off, not like a gazelle, more like a soldier marching up the pyramid.

I went back into the air conditioning and ordered a cappuccino. To think things over. There was this good guy that I had become. I knew guys were not good. They do good things. And sometimes bad things. I thought my way through a whole cappuccino and a pair of churros, too. But I was glad she put me on the good side again. Even if it was a half lie.

I finished in time to see her waving from a pyramid peak. I could not quite make out her face—I would have needed a telescope for that—but I was betting she had one of those silly grins mountain climbers and tourists get when they stand on the top of something.

I had forgotten how easy it was to get wide-eyed when you visit Oaxaca. I was not jaded about the place, but I had gotten past the gaga stage. I was in love with the city.

I looked back at Randy. She was tiny. The ruins were big, bigger than the Zócalo with its Cathedral and City Hall. Randy would be at it a while, so I took my normal post, the one where I sat under a big tree, some say three hundred years old, when my visitors went exploring. All I cared about was no sun getting through its hundred feet of leaves and the breeze blowing through underneath. I got another cappuccino, too.

In an hour and a half, she came back reddish from the sun. Not glowing scarlet like the most clueless tourists who did full lobster burns. Hers was more of a pink shrimp bake, lightly toasting the foggy indoor pale she had brought from San Francisco.

She had a juice in the café with me and talked history. I could not get her to talk about herself. Or even her problem. She was into these pyramids. She had done her homework and told me things I did not know. Monte Albán was bustling about the same time as Rome. Forty thousand lived up where the ruins are now, and many more passed through, trading everything from feathers and jaguar skins to obsidian–the rocks they made sharp knives and war axes with. It was the New York or–you have to say it–the ancient Rome of Mexico.

I had been thinking about more recent history, like when my bakery turned into ruins with explosion and bulldozer help. No tourists went there.

She went to a vending machine and bought a water bottle along with some kind of energy bar. She did not need it. She still had the just-arrived rush that keeps you going for a day or two. But she slowed down after that bar and did her serious look, the one I remembered, the one she always had, ever since she was a couple of weeks old, a little cross-eyed and with no smile. She started talking problem.

"You know Oaxaca and the people. I have a problem. I need help. Santo Gordo help."

I did the father thing. Fathers say they will help and sometimes do. I was planning to try. If I could not be Santo Gordo for my daughter, then my sainthood would be revoked.

"You know I work with charities, groups that do good." She said good with quotes and capital letters. "I do communications for nonprofits in a big umbrella group. But one nonprofit doesn't seem right. It sent pictures to put up on its pages, but these pictures were taken from other sites, from other charities. It didn't respond when I asked about it. I think it's a scam. It has its tax ID, but for its references, everyone is off on some sort of research junket, and I can't get in touch to confirm anything."

She whipped out a small computer from her purse and showed me the name, "Food for All," on a web page, all done up in a fancy logo, with two skinny, curly F's all wrapped around a fat looking A, and then she showed me another simpler version, "FfA," its short hip name typed out in some snappy looking letters. She showed me pictures–a storehouse full of food, a truck unloading on a dirt road next to adobe brick houses, people smiling as they ate from clay bowls, children drinking something gooey.

The site had two names as references, a doctor and a college professor, and, of course, a place to give your credit card donation.

"We built the site for them. We did the logo. We do not want to be associated with a scam. But we do not want to pull a site down without proof."

She showed me other charity sites with pictures, the same pictures as at the FfA site. "Someone copied these photos for FfA. Maybe it is on the up and up and someone just took a stupid shortcut, but I doubt it. Everyone has a camera, and the Internet is everywhere for uploads. Even you send me pictures sometimes. If this person is running a scam, he is stupid. I did a couple of easy searches and found more duplicates. Does he think we're as stupid as he is?"

She had an address in Oaxaca. I don't know how she got it. I did not ask, but she had friends. The address was up the street. The middle-class part of Oaxaca was small, where we gringos infiltrate into and live. I would check it out.

"And I think this person is American. Someone who could get the paperwork for the tax ID, who could find an expert reference that would be going away for a year or so. I think this is something he might have done over and over, never a big kill, but a living income, maybe a good one, especially if he lives in Mexico." She had analyzed this scam pretty well.

Now was time for action. What would Santo Gordo do? He was the expat dumb enough to get hit in the head, dumb enough to follow thugs around after they blew up buildings. He would take on this guy. He was dumb enough for something like that.

But Roberto, the other half of me, wanted to stay home and take it easy. Roberto would look on the web a little. Roberto would telephone Efraím. But he would keep his head covered. Not like a saint.

I knew deep inside Santo Gordo would be giving this FfA place a visit. Easy-going Roberto would be off dreaming of comida but he would make sure a couple of taxistas and maybe the Señora provided backup.

"We need to stop this, but if word gets out about a scam, then donations stop for every charity, for the charities doing wonderful work. So I need it undercover. I need it quiet. Isn't that what you do, Santo Gordo, Señor detective, Dad?"

****

I had some time to myself the next morning, Randy was going to do business with Lupe that day, lawyer business, working on the settlement money from Beto's biological, kidnapping, rich, dead-beat father. Randy wanted to get the payments legal and locked in, with everything protected in a trust that paid out to mom Lupe and sent baby Beto to school. And make it something that a local village guy could not marry away from her. Lupe would be ripe for marriage to the wrong sort when she had a fat, all-dollar bank account. Randy had set up a settlement money spigot running for Lupe, but not flooding her, one with an initial spurt for a house or maybe a business, and then a reasonable drain for living and good schools, and finally doing a big splash when Beto goes to college and heads out on his own.

Randy would explain this to the Señora. Lupe now had money. She was not the servant any longer. Lupe was a *señora* too. I did not know what that would do to the house relations. But that was later. Today was my FfA time. Other business would wait. Even Efraím and his bakery would have to wait another day.

No big online directories in Oaxaca told you who lived where. You needed to walk around to find someone, not search on the internet. I could not just look up the address that Randy had given me and see who lived there. It would take a little detective work to find Randy's nonprofit criminal.

I went to the address. It was a doorway in a wall, like ones everywhere, a yellow wall, covered with flowers like most walls. I walked into the park across the street from the door. And tried to look touristy.

I liked this park, a little one, a block square, with fountains and benches, with a *torta* stand on one corner and mezcal-tasting shop on another, just right for a quick rest. My day would not be quick, though. Gumshoeing takes time.

I looked for a fake reason to be there, something people would believe was real. I was in luck. A shoeshine boy, maybe ten, small for his age, carried his wooden box with a handle that doubled as a footrest, and walked toward me. My shoes were big and leather. They had gotten a dusting when the bakery fell on me. Lots of scrapes and dirt on the toes. I had a plan.

I sat on a bench so I could see the door. The boy was on his way over before I could wave. We bargained. I wanted an hour-long supershine. He said he would make my shoes happy. He opened the box, helped me lift my left foot on to the footrest, and placed some plastic inserts inside my shoe next to my ankle to keep my sock clean. He did not worry about shoe polish on him. In fact, he started rubbing it on with two stained fingers right after he did a long shoe scrub with some suspicious soapy water that he squirted from an old plastic water bottle

While he was busy, I had lots of time to look at the doorway. A shoeshine could last almost forever if your shoes were a mess. These shoeguys had their pride and would not stop until the shoes came close to mirror status. I was lucky. Mine looked like hundred-year-old road worker shoes, except in Oaxaca those guys wore homemade sandals, not shoes, ones with toes sticking out, waiting for an accident.

My shine was going to cost about two dollars, with tip. Easy, cheap detectiving while I watched over the boy's head. Nothing happened at the door.

After about a thousand slaps with his rag, my shoes shined like the sun. The door in the wall stayed the same, shut. My first stakeout ploy was over. The boy left happy with the tip. I admired my shoes for five minutes, peeking up at the doorway every ten seconds or so. I needed to think of something else to do, some cover thing. Deep cover is what they call it in spy books. I could not be the

Santo Gordo of Oaxaca. I needed to be a clueless, anonymous tourist. That sounds easy. The clueless part was.

I paced around the park like it was an archeological site under inspection. It was pretty, it was a gem, but no one studied it, they just walked through it and sometimes sat in the shade. In the corners couples stopped and got into heavy kissing. In the grass between the walkways locals played with their dogs, but this was not a tourist destination park. It was more like an extra living room where you went to let the world drift around you while you sat in the shade for an hour or two.

I walked up to a statue of the guy the park was named for and studied the plaque underneath. I read it for fifteen minutes. It was three lines long, but lined up exactly with my suspect's wall and door. I walked around the park, trying out its short little walks. It was divided up like some geometric puzzle. You could take different paths and look at the flowers and fountains, but the park was only one block long and one block wide. After an hour people were looking at me–I could tell. I was not being anonymous. I was not being normal. I needed something any expat would do, something that took time.

I looked around. Couples were here and there, not quite coupling, but getting close, as they spread themselves on the benches and grass. Most were teens, doing lip-locks and sitting in each other's laps. It was an afterschool thing; it was a holiday thing, too, but any time was after school in Oaxaca with sessions in the morning and in the afternoon and some at night. I watched the couples. Some looked around, like they were checking out other possibilities even in heavy clenches. Some looked deep in love with eyes smashed shut. Some just looked busy.

I figured I better quit looking. You had to pretend couples were not there. You looked above, behind, and past them. They could stay in the park for hours, but I could not try that cover, doing a smoochfest, even if I could find a kisser to sit on the bench with me. Gringos did it in their rooms.

Then I saw the way. A man my age, American, straw hat, glasses, short sleeves, khaki trousers–my uniform–sat on a bench, staring intently, waiting for a webpage to load on his laptop. The city had hung little black boxes with wires coming out up on the trees to put in Wi-Fi, or as they call it, "wee fee." Most people only used it when they were desperate. The connection was slow enough to for you to nap or maybe do a full siesta waiting to look up something. It was perfect.

I went home and grabbed my laptop. It was old, ugly, and slow like me, a match for the wee fee.

I went back and sat on a bench facing the wall with the suspect's door. I watched it looking over the laptop screen. Now I just had to figure out my bathroom and snack situation, and I would be set for the day. I couldn't use a coffee cup like detective cops in the movies. And I had no idea what the poor country people did here. I did not want to know. They did not have enough money to go anywhere with a *baño*. I was not brave enough to look behind the trees to find out. But my tank was not yet full, so I had time to work it out.

E-mail finally loaded in fifteen minutes. I looked, nothing new. Offers for cheap prepaid cremations were the latest junk mail hitting my old-man demographic these days, that, and the always popular ED pills from Canada, along with gun people wanting me to sign petitions to shoot things down in Congress.

I clicked on a newspaper bookmark for the official news here. It gave me another quarter hour to watch the door while it loaded. Its news was full of speeches from the Oaxaca State Governor and every minor and major official around. Perfect—nothing interesting to distract me from the door. Then I got the alert, battery low. Ten minutes of computer left. I put it on sleep.

I pretended it was working. No one noticed. Just another crazy gringo writing food reviews on Facebook or updating his Oaxaca blog with pictures of cute little kids in funny-looking outfits to show the folks back home. I had found my cover, an old gringo, putting in his computer time until he died or went back north. Two hours went by.

The door in the wall cracked opened. I jerked up straight. Two boys came out, Oaxaca schoolboys in scout uniforms with their backpacks. They looked around and pushed the door fully open. A car waited behind it. A red one. A woman, maybe thirties, Oaxacan for sure, was driving. Blue blouse, sun glasses. High heels too, I bet. I was enjoying myself. I took notes. The car backed out, one kid got in, the other started closing the big metal door in the wall.

For a minute I could see through the doorway. Two stories of apartments, maybe six or seven all together, and underneath them, cars. Your basic up-to-date, modernized Oaxaca courtyard complex. Lots of them were around. Not just one family lived there. According to Randy, her American crook lived there, too.

I was looking for an American doing a scam. Probably living in Mexico so he could get away fast and leave no trace, then do it somewhere else with a new scam. That was what I would have done. But I was leaving the thinking to Randy on this case. I was gumshoeing, only.

OK, the woman was not Randy's crook, but it wouldn't hurt to know more. I held on to the laptop with my busted arm and fished for my phone. I took a pic and then another of her fancy new VW. With the license plate showing. I could blow it up just like in the movies.

The boy climbed into the car. They drove off. I sat there looking at my pictures. And the license plate.

It was from up north in Puebla, but that was not a surprise. Most people register their car in some state where fees are cheap. No penalty for that, just a little bribe now and then to keep everything running. The Governor says he is stopping petty offences like these, but they work too well to ever stop. Drivers get cheap car registrations and police get a chance for a little bite, what they call the *mordida*, not a shark bite, more like the insect bites that annoy and can go on and on, but never are bad enough for you to do much but scratch now and then.

Bribes are part of the culture. The government does not have to pay much salary when cops can be small-scale entrepreneurs–that is the hot word Americans and Mexico City are pushing these days.

Here in Mexico everything is a crime, but one that is easy to ignore. You tell a little lie for cheap license plates. And have a handful of pesos to fix a speeding ticket. That sounds as fair to as paying some off-the-wall driving school to erase your all-American bad driving points. Here the payoff is simple, quick, and direct, just between you, the cop and your conscience.

A tap on the head and I jumped. I was caught.

"Hi, Dad." Randy had me.

"You would make a great detective, Randy." I did not tell her she could make a great assassin, too, sneaking up like that. She scared me enough to make me head to the hotel for a quick *baño* visit.

I hotfooted toward the hotel and called back, "Just in time, Randy. Watch that door" I took off like some kid holding on to himself, but doing it slyly with the laptop, heading to the hotel located between the tortas and the mezcal.

I gave the waiter there a couple of pesos. He let me in, and all went fine. Actually it took a little talking, and I only had a twenty, but it was worth it. I was back to the park in five minutes.

"I could see you waiting here from the balcony. What are you doing pacing around?" Randy greeted me rapid fire when I got back. "Is that the place?"

Of course she knew it was the place. The street name was up on the wall, and the number was big enough to be an eye chart. And everyone could hear us. A few people were looking. No one cared, but they might soon. I needed to be touristy and redirect Randy a little.

"Want to chat?" It worked. We sat. I could watch the door over her head.

Randy pried everything that had happened in the park out of me. I was pretty priable to her. I told her I was waiting to see who came out and about the shoeshine and the computer and woman with the red car. She smiled, stood up, and walked to the door in the wall.

I started to yell, but that just make the whole thing less detective-like. Randy yelled first, anyway. She was loud and called up to a woman who looked out over the roof terrace wall. A dog looked down at us too and had a barking fit, the normal thing roof dogs do in Oaxaca. They never jump off, or at least I have never seen one do that. The woman calmed him. "¡Perro, cálmate! No ladres, Elvis."

Elvis–nice Mexican name for a dog. The dog went back to his normal guard spot on the corner and lay down.

"*¿Señora, por favor, podría ayudarme?*"–Can you help me? Randy's Spanish was good. She kept going. "I am on a visit from the United States, and I understand a famous American artist lives here."

"The Americans here are not artists. They are old men. Unless drinking is art."

"Do you know their names? I think he has given up painting but he was famous before."

Randy was the direct action part of the family. I was more the cagey detective, doing the sneaking around work. Her style worked fine. Probably better than mine.

"Señor Abrams lives in apartment five and Señor Davis in nine. One is tall, the other fat. I feed them sometimes. One eats, the other does not. They feed my dog sometimes.

But they are gone for the day. One left early and the other left late."

"That is not the name I am looking for. I am sorry. I must have the wrong address. Thank you, Señora."

Randy waved goodbye. Randy smiled at me, looking like she just won the Indy 500. She walked up to me.

"Now you heard the names. Do you know the men?" She asked me like she was in charge. Well she was–it was her crook, not mine.

"You know expats mostly by their first name in Oaxaca. That and where they come from. I am Roberto from Baltimore. You are going to be Randita from San Fran."

"I will be Randy Evans."

I let that ruffled feather lay itself back down and went back to the main topic. "I'll find out who he is. I can check in the library. Everyone registers to get books. Well, everybody I know does."

That would give me a chance to get away from there and think up a better cover, especially if I did not know this guy.

Randy looked at the door and then down towards me. "Let's get some lunch first. Any recommendations?"

She was my kind of detective.

****

It was not a big lunch that I had with Randy. Not a *comida grande*. That was what I called the lunch I normally ate.

I had a beer and a torta filled with good soft cheese and bad commercial ham. Randy got something vegetarian. That meant lots of beans in most places, but in this restaurant they had cactus leaf salad.

Even worse, broccoli, that weird euro-import, was trying to push out cactus leaves. It had made its entrée in what were otherwise traditional restaurants. They tried to put it on my plate. I did not like this global veggie world moving in, but as long as they kept the old food, too, I would not protest much.

We were eating in the hotel with the *baño* that saved me a few minutes earlier. They had adapted to the times and that meant veggies. I figured I was one of the last gringos alive who was not wolfing down leaves and flowers.

I could watch the door in the wall on the other side of the park out the restaurant window. It was a block away but I could see it had stayed shut. Randy was ready to run if someone came out, ready to give a snap with the camera. But knowing her, she would probably tie the guy to a tree before I got there.

I kept lunch light so I would not need a nap, and Randy kept it light because that was what she did. We talked about what to do next when we found the guy. We were not sure and decided to find him first, then figure it out.

Randy said she had more work to do. She could not help me any more just then. She had to go back to the lawyer's

135

office. I headed back to my park bench, carrying my dead laptop.

Before I got across the street and after Randy turned the corner, two young guys walked up. Bristleheads, hair trimmed short, like workers do sometimes, wearing old work clothes, handmade sandals and long sleeve shirts. No one wears long sleeves except businessmen under their suit coats and school kids getting indoctrinated in the working clothes they would wear the rest of their lives, clothes from the north and too hot for Oaxaca.

"*Ayúdenos, Señor Santo*"–help us. They sounded like they were begging but they had me by the shoulders leading me to an old Volkswagen. One helped me in the front with a push that tried to be gentle, but he did not seem to know gentle. I fell against the seat.

This was not good. We headed down by the river. We passed some cabs, and I was ready to yell, but the driver gave me a don't-do-that look. I sat still and watched closely. It was them, the spikehair, dagger-arm guys. Dripping blood. Blowing up things. But with long sleeves and no hair. We were off for a ride. Not good.

"Señor Santo, you must help us. Your crazy friend Efraím is after us. He has his taxista friends everywhere. We cannot go home. His friends would see us. We cannot work. Our mothers are crying. Our wives are angry. Our sisters are yelling on the phone. Our sick father is mad and beating his head on the wall. You must help us."

Efraím was not crazy. But he could be scary.

"We can tell him who gave us the money. We can tell him. It was all an accident. My knife slipped. I was just

136

waving it a little, and it went after the hose by itself. Knives do that. They like to cut things."

This sounded like a threat, but the guy was crying. I was ready to scream, but I fought it. I sat still.

"Who paid you?" I tried for my detective voice, but it was an octave too high.

"Tell your friend Efraím we can meet and work this out. We do not want the money. We are innocent. A gringo called us and promised us a job if we would just give someone, the bakery man, a good talk, a stern one, maybe threaten some. And show the bakery man our thousand-dollar, LA tattoos that we got before Uncle Sam sent us home. But my knife went crazy and cut the hose. Now the gringo will not pay because he said we made a mess. And I got burned. Do you want to see the burns?"

"You want to see my broken arm?" I started to wave the cast at him but remembered I was scared.

He raised his hand in front of my face, red and covered in some kind of grease. "You need a doctor. I will contact Efraím. Let me out and I will call him. I will make him understand."

"You promised, Señor Santo. We will call you. We know your number. We know about you, sitting in the park and watching all day. We are simple workers here. We are poor workers who are innocent. The knife is guilty. I will give it to you."

He pulled it out. It was one that folded. It was big, about the size of a three-pound *guajolote* turkey leg, gold on the ends, with some kind of animal horn in the middle. But mostly it was big. He reached over slowly–I jumped about a foot–and he handed me his guilty knife.

"You go. Your friend's cabstand is over there. Take him the guilty knife. Talk to him."

I was out fast. I walked to the corner with my best high step. I did not look back, but I remembered it was a blue VW bug, like a thousand others. It would be hard to find. But Efraím would. I was sure.

****

He was sitting in his cab talking on his cell. I was huffing, hot footing up the street. Efraím started making motions–calm down; I started making motions–hurry up.

"Come here, quick." My voice had stayed high-pitched. It was shaky too.

He pulled the cab out of the line and drove towards me, flashing his lights. I got in.

"Mi amigo, what is wrong?" He looked concerned after seeing my eyeballs jumping out of my head.

"They had me. The spikehairs–now they are shaveheads. They had me in their car and kidnapped me." He looked at me like he was searching for stigmata and other wounds, things you would look for when the dead rose. I was not built like I could escape alive from thugs muscled up as much as those two.

"They pulled a knife on me. Here it is." I handed him the knife.

"You escaped? You took away their knife?" His eyes were bigger than mine now. I had never seen Efraím amazed before. Next time will be when the angels carry to him upstairs to see his other saint friend, Peter, at the gate.

"No, they gave it to me. To give to you. Here it is."

"Was it a warning?" I will find them and they will wish…"

"No, they want to talk. They were scared. They said you were hunting them. They can't go home. Their wives are angry."

"They had better be scared."

My phone rang.

It was them. I handed it to Efraím. He said, "Talk." That was it.

I could hear their tiny voices. I could not understand, only hear the pleading tone. Efraím muttered every foul word in Spanish that I ever heard. Their pleading went higher pitched. Efraím yelled back. I decided to let them work it out and got out and leaned on the door. The phone went silent, and he threw it out the window. It bounced on the sidewalk. I picked it up and looked at Efraím. He sat there staring straight ahead. That lasted for a minute. I looked away, looked at the trees, the sky, the people standing waiting for a cab. He was not in a mood for communicating.

"Get in." He was trying to be civil but something had snapped.

"Hijos de la chingada. Virgen Santa." I sat down and stayed quiet. I shook my phone, the one Efraím threw. It was still

alive. I wondered if the two bristleheads would be much longer.

We drove off. Efraím went on for a while, and I learned some new things to say in Spanish, new ways to mix sex and religion when you are angry. "They are my cousin's sons. They are my shithead, *pinche cabrón* cousin's sons." He put in some English this time.

That was all he said as we drove back to the Centro, past the Zócalo and up the crowded afternoon street toward my part of town.

"I have to think. Those two were always trouble after my cousin got sick and could not father them well. I should have stepped in. They are family. I must watch out for them. I did not know they were back from el Norte. They were cooks in LA and caught in a raid. And sent back. I did not know they were here.

"So they were not from Mexico City." Tío Franciso, the bakery owner, had said that, up at his house. That was what I had thought too.

Efraím did not pay attention to me. "They were corrupted. I could hear it in their voices. LA is hell for men when they go north. They go crazy. They stay crazy. They bring crazy home. Gang crazy. Gun crazy. Knife crazy. Tattoo crazy."

"What do we do?"

"You do not worry. They are my cousin's sons. I will take care of them. They need our family's strength. My cousin has been sick for ten years. I will see their family and we will decide what to do."

140

This complicated things, but it made it easier too. I did not have to worry about those two. Whether they were going to show up in the *Sección Roja* in the newspapers with holes in them. Whether they were going to be on my conscience. Whether they would count against my sainthood.

"They said they got a call from an American, trying to pretend he was Mexican. Can you believe that? Said he was from Mexico City."

That city seems to be getting all the blame.

"They told me that the American was going to give them two thousand pesos to talk to the bakery owner. They did not know the owner was family. Stupid, tattooed, *malditos desgraciados.*"

I could think of nothing to say. Efraím was using me as a friend to talk at, not one to talk to. I stayed quiet.

"They arranged it all on the phone with this American. And a Mexican they met up with later under Benito Juarez's feet on the hill, the one you saw. Probably the one that came first to make the offer for the bakery. He gave those two a message, keep quiet, no money." He really was from Mexico City, they said. He was a messenger who did not know anything." Efraím laughed. It was not a good laugh.

"No one knows anything." That was my contribution to the conversation. It did not calm Efraím.

"I know what I am going to do." He pounded his fist on his little fancy steering wheel. The Virgin Mary over the horn jumped. Me too.

That ended the conversation. He drove silently and left me at my apartment. I shook his hand, but he was off somewhere else in his head.

"We will talk more later." That was it. He drove away.

I decided not to go home. I needed my espresso place. I needed my mezcal place too.

I took a table by the window. People walked by like just like was a normal day. Then my phone rang again.

It was them.

"We forgot." They sounded more alive. But still scared. "You must tell Efraím. When the gringo called to set up the deal, he was in the Llano Park. We are sure." That was the park a block away. Where I always went.

"How do you know?"

"We could hear a speech in the background. The one from the demonstration with loudspeakers. The farmers." I remembered that day. It was a couple weeks back. I walked by. Hundreds of men in white outfits with old sandals and straw hats stood around and waved homemade signs. They wanted their river back. I did not know who had it, but I was betting it was someone with money and maybe a factory. They came in pickups, ten or twenty men and women to a truck, and stayed all day making speeches. But they did not block the road. That was what I remembered.

"He must have been on a payphone in the park. It did not sound like a cell phone. You must tell Efraím. And did you give Efraím the knife? It is the guilty one."

"And we are sorry, we have your computer. We will bring it to you."

"I did not want to get into niceties with them. "Give it to the Señora where I live, and I will tell Efraím about the call. Goodbye."

I did not call Efraím right away. I just let the mezcal sink in and then diluted it with espresso.

The phone rang again. I was ready to yell at the two. But caught myself as I heard another voice.

Christ, it was Randy. I had forgotten her.

****

I told Randy I was on the way to the library to check on her two bad guys. I thanked her for her good work on getting their names that morning in the park. I did not tell her about my other two bad guys, Efraím's cousins-once-removed, or something like that. I wanted to keep his secret for a while. Maybe forever.

I was remembering to be nice. Something I did not have to do when I was alone. It was not coming easy. I was getting old. Or maybe I was still scared after the kidnapping and the phone call.

When I got there, the library was about to reopen after its siesta time. It had learned to take a break in the afternoon a long time ago. This version of your basic American public library had embraced some Mexican ways of doing things. It had its little coffee shop and reading room just like in the States, but also a big open Mexican courtyard. The old rooms around it overflowed with books, as they should when there were more books than shelves. And like public libraries in the States, it thought about people as much as books. It tried to do good, the capital G kind of good, both for expats who needed a break from Mexico and for Mexicans to help them learn some American words and ways. For poor Mexicans who could not visit, the library went to them with books and food drives and volunteers. Yep, it did good, and did not scare away too many Mexicans, except when the place celebrated the Fourth too loud and local people worried if it was another American invasion.

Patrons read or played cards and sometimes did tourist tours or listened to lectures. Mexicans joined them in *entrevistas*, the you-speak-your language, I-speak-mine kind of one-on-ones to practice a new language. I tried it once and got a bar owner from the tourist area as my partner. He wanted to learn new words for new drinks. I knew beer and was learning mezcal. He wanted mojitos and fancy weird fruit Martinis, I knew little about martinis and had never heard of mojitos. I had done scotch and rum and coke when I was young. That was my generation. Martinis, they were my father's. I had watched him make them in a metal shaker when I was a kid, but his were not fancy fruit things, they were pretty much straight gin. So I did not have much to talk about. After a couple sessions he went back to his bar and that was it. My first social try ended, and I returned to books, not people.

Many American men and women came and had conversations, but ones in English. You could buy a cup of coffee, sit, and chat up anyone. For me, the library's big sin was no espresso. That limited my socializing. People brewed weak sipping coffee there. I had gone local for the strong stuff.

Four of us stood waiting at the door–well, not really a door, more a gate to the courtyard. I could see in through the bars. It was cool and dark inside. Outside we leaned into the shadows of the afternoon to keep the sun away. It would not be long. The library ran on gringo time, the kind a clock keeps, not the kind Oaxacan people keep in their heads when they are sleepy from a siesta. That meant just enough wait for a drop or two of sweat, not a shirtful.

We were quite the gang waiting at the gate. I had my scar and my cast. One guy was pacing back and forth–he needed his book fix. We need a the rehab spa to help the world's book junkies, scouring shelves, hoping for something they had missed before, posting all over the internet when they found a good author. I was a little like him but knew I could quit if I had to.

The two women with us were coming to socialize and sit. That was pretty addicting, too. It happened as much as reading. Then two more walked up. They were the volunteers. People got hooked on volunteering, too.

Finally a woman from inside opened the gate. We took our places. Mine was in front of the checkout lady, Susan. She wore a nametag but I knew her anyway.

I played detective and tried out one of the names that Randy's yelling had gotten.

"Hola, Susan, I am looking for Señor Abrams. I thought he was going to be here this afternoon."

145

"Oh you mean Stan." The woman volunteering looked at me funny. "Come on, Roberto, why so formal?"

Everyone knew each other. It was small town America in Oaxaca. You used first names. You nodded hello to expats, and you heard everything about everyone, except when he was a crook.

"I am switching to Mexican, formal last-naming when I talk. I might just shake your hand and call you Señora." I still did not know her last name.

She shook her head.

"Stan usually hangs out over at the Perro Verde Café."

I thanked her, tipped my hat at the others, sort of formally, and headed there. It was not far, near the old theater. The dead one. A Cineplex with ten screens opened in the shopping mall out towards the airport, so this theater got boarded up. I remembered the premall days when I saw a film inside, a long time back. I do not know the movie name–I did not know any Spanish then–but I remember the heat and the fans drowning out everything, except they could not blow away the cloud of perfume that hung over the seats. There were no scent-free zones in Oaxaca.

The new shopping center theater was air-conditioned but could have been found in Anyplace, USA,–just a big box with doors. Expats went but kept their eyes closed when they entered, pretending they were still in real Oaxaca.

The old dead theater building first became a church, a bible-beating, old-time Protestant one, not Catholic. That failed, and the place turned into a big kung fu classroom, but one with a floor that sloped down toward the screen.

146

That failed. Now there was a little store in front and boarded over windows in the back.

The Perro Verde was across the street. Che stared out from one wall, and a mural of Zapata sitting on a tricked-out bicycle looked down from the other.

Revolutionary style meant something in Mexico–Zapata echoed in the voices for change that you heard every day–but this was a hangout for middle-class students, not firebrands. Tables were teenage sticky and had pink or blue ratty-haired kids bent over laptop screens, just as they should. This place could have been anywhere–Berkeley, Europe, and maybe now in China, too.

Some were reading books, but laptops were in the majority. The young crowd sipped away, mostly espresso, but wine, too. The place was too arty, too youthful, and too hip for me to be a regular, but they did make good espresso. That was what I had heard.

Stan sat in the back. I never thought of him as arty. And youth was something neither of us could remember well.

"Hi, Stan. You mind?"

He nodded, and I pulled up a stool. Stan was the skinny one that Randy found out about. Tall, too. His knees banged against the little table, moving it when he slid over to make room for me. He was reading a Mexican weekly, the intelligent guy's news report. No pictures of dead people, no government speeches, no society photos in fancy gowns. Just essays. The right paper for an older thinker. Kids would have something more revolutionary.

"Roberto, what brings you here? I thought you lived at La Avenida."

Everyone knew Santo Gordo's hangout, especially after the bakery blew. Stan put down his paper. The table wobbled, but he caught it with his knees wedged underneath and saved his coffee from tipping. He looked like he had a lot of experience in table management.

"I'm looking for something new. With my bakery exploded, I need a new home. They have a pastelería around the corner so this might be it." There was a pastelería around almost every corner in Oaxaca.

I ordered. Stan sipped.

"You recovered."

I waved my arm in the cast at him. "But the head is ok." I tapped my head above my ear with the cast and it made a good thump, a little too hard. "That was what my doc said. I miss my bakery, though. It had the worst injuries."

"What happened when it came down with you in it, anyway?"

"I learned a lot. Don't mess with old, blown up buildings, even if there might be some donuts in the back." The story was out that I was hunting for donuts when it collapsed.

We went on talking about the explosion. I watched him closely. He did not flinch, stutter, or hesitate. He looked innocent—no nervousness, no jumpiness in his answers. Stan was not good at holding back, at doing anything Gary Cooper-ish, and he was a blubberer, too. He cried at movies, I heard—I was ready to scratch him off my suspect list. But first I did a little more questioning.

"How is that place you live in working out?"

"You mean the court. That is what we call it. Dan and me. He has a place upstairs, I like it. A good mix of people. I think the locals like us two gringos."

I did not tell him what the woman said to Randy about them, but the important thing was Dan lived there, too. But Dan was a more improbable suspect than Stan. I could not see him setting up some complicated scam. Dan was flaky, like his Alzheimer's peaked early. He would forget to show up, or you would see him wandering in the park. Not wandering around like me, but like someone really lost.

Those two were off the hook. I had thought I was getting somewhere when I found Stan, but struck out.

"The Court, that's what Dan and I call the place where we live, is a lot better now that Frank left. He was the noisy one and got the Mexicans teed off. He left because it was too expensive, that was what he said. Four-fifty a month for an apartment–too expensive? Could you ever do that in the states? With a terrace?"

"What happened?" I was casual, cool, like Paul Newman playing poker, not my normal self. Stan did not pay any attention. He just liked to talk.

"Frank left the court and moved down to the other side of the Zócalo. Down on the way to the river, near the old railroad tracks."

That was the cheap side of town. This was getting interesting.

"You know we do not say bad things about expats here, but that guy was creepy. Things are good in the apartments now that he is gone."

We talked more. I did not want it to look like I was too interested in Frank, so I brought up other things. We went on about New Year's Eve coming the next day. Everyone had plans. Restaurants offered specials with a DJ, drinks, and meals. And noise, way too much for me. But you had to do it, you had to go out with friends. Stan invited me to join in with a gang from the library. I told him I had other plans with my daughter. I knew the Señora was having a big cena for the night, and we were expected. That was fine with me. Only rockets there, not DJs.

It was time to get back to Frank.

"Where exactly did that Frank go anyway?" Not the cleanest segue ever, but I made my move. "I might need something cheaper someday." That greased the transition.

"Someplace near the big market by the railroad tracks. Where the little buses, the *colectivos*, leave from. Near a stone church. Frank told me that they had a place with cheap apartments opening down there. One for gringos like him. I would not want to live there."

That helped. The bus stop helped more than the stone church. Churches were on every other corner, just like the pastelerías.

I got out quick after that. Dan gave me a *"hasta luego."* I gave him a Oaxaca manhug, with a backslap, but I had to watch that cast. It could make a backslap painful.

I had made a detective score. I was excited.

Now where was that damn stone church? I called Efraím. Taxistas knew all the buildings of Oaxaca. It was pretty much where Stan had said. About a mile walk. I was up for it. My detective rush after getting the location had me ready for anything.

I went into a joy bubble. I don't know what else to call it. The day looked bright. I was happy. I was a detective first class.

OK, I did not have a plan, but I did not care. It was a great day, not too hot. A breeze was blowing. Some clouds passed over, shielding me every couple of minutes, big puffy ones that blossomed out, and you could see them churning if you stayed still and watched. I did not have the time.

I started at a pretty good clip and headed south. I got to the fancy concert hall, the one in all the post cards showing its loopy French-architecture curlicues from a century ago, the hall where the local middle class celebrates, but the gringos go, too, for string quartet concerts. Oaxacan export singers fly in from NYC to lead a protest and do a show there, and opera is broadcast live from New York. It saves the expats from going to Mexico City when they need a culture shot—that is, the big Western Civ culture. Indigenous culture down here hooks Americans, and they become experts in rugs and dyes and woodcarving, but they need to come up for air and get a dose of Big Apple culture every month or two. The concert hall does that for them.

Then down the street, I passed one of my favorite shops, the doll shop, full of heads. You name a head, and they have it. Pink heads, brown heads, black heads, blue heads. You could do a Frankenstein and stick one on any doll body. They had rows of bodies and wigs and a box of eyeballs. I felt like a surgeon whenever I walked by. Or a horror writer.

Then on the other side of the street, more dolls. But these were the baby Jesuses, ones for the posadas and Noche Buena. They dressed better than anyone else in Oaxaca. The Señora's Jesus came from there. Lots of velvet and lace and collars, looking ready for Rembrandt to come by and put them in a museum painting. They looked wrong for Christmas to us gringos. We wanted reindeer and Santa suits and naked Jesus dolls getting swaddled. But we were adapting.

I enjoyed the walk. I did not think much about looking for a criminal. I felt the breeze, stayed in the shade, and wandered. Mostly going south, but turning when something was interesting.

I passed a bakery. It was worth a close look. I bought a churro and chewed at it as I left, wondering how they got the exact right amount of grease and sugar suspended in the dough when they made a good one. This one was good. It lasted just past the door.

Then in a couple of blocks, I passed three preschools bursting with kids. Preschools were everywhere, like churches. Mexico had more kids per square mile than anywhere, usually in schoolrooms covered with *Winipooh* pictures, along with his friend Sponge Bob, the guy who invaded Mexico with the latest batch of us Americans.

The blocks were getting grittier. The graffiti had layers. The earliest were roundish, doughlike letters forming words no one could figure out. Except the gang members who sprayed them on. The top layers were spikey. Maybe the painters changed drugs? Like they were into something jangly and scary. Just right for down here by the tracks.

This part of town was not mine. I was from up the hill. Near my parks. This side of the city was drive-through territory for us expats.

I got to the stone church. I started looking around. Checking the layout.

A little plaza, one full of sun, not trees, lay in front of the church. I sat on a bench to reconnoiter. The place was surrounded by ten-foot walls, like everywhere. But these walls were not antique treasures like up where I lived. They were just run down.

The plaza looked like a high-wire act gone bad with wires dangling from cement utility poles all around. Residents had tapped into the electricity and hung quick connections everywhere.

It was harder to tap in up near the Señora's. Up there, utilities were buried so tourists could see colonial buildings without 20th-century clutter. It helped business. And looked good in the photos. You had to go in a manhole and fight the rats for a power connection in my neighborhood. People still did it, but not as often as often.

The power poles were the norm—short, thin ones in this dry country, not enough wood, so cement had to do. Short enough so I could reach up and almost touch the wires. But the pole was thick enough to hold notices. A couple were stuck up with tape and not too old.

I went over. "For rent Rooms con baño y luz"– inexpensive living for Americans, what Frank had found. There was an address, no phone. You could get more rent from us Americans than from the locals, even from my Frank suspect. I wrote down the address in my brain. It was on the other side of the square. About where Stan had said.

Under the apartment notice, I saw another flyer, one I had never seen before. Usually flyers got posted for lost dogs and cats, and sometimes a missing cellphone or even a teen-age girl. This was different.

It was in good Spanish and got to the heart of many bad relationships down here, "It is ten PM. Do you know where your husband is? Professional Detection Services."

It had a drawing of a video camera on one side and a big eye looking through a magnifying glass on the other.

Detective competition. That was fine with me. I used my good arm and pulled off a number—it had those little tear offs cut into the bottom of the posting. I could use some help down in this neighborhood.

I wanted to keep an eye on this room for rent, and I was too obvious. People were already looking at me. I needed a local guy, but I did not want to bring Efraím in on this yet. I wanted to check it out first. Maybe with some so-called professional help.

It was not far across the plaza to the rooms for rent. The door was shut. I went back into the plaza. From there I could see the door fine, but I was the only gringo in a couple of blocks. I was not worried about being safe at that time of day, just about sticking out. It was time for a phone call. I pulled out the slip of paper and called a professional.

****

I met Edgar, the professional, that night. He was the guy with the flyer showing a video camera and magnifying glass.

I was lucky to find him. Serendipity happens sometimes, like finding his note next to the room ad. Serendipity is important, maybe more important than anything else. In the library you come across books. In travel you stumble into places. In life you bump into a new friends or maybe a wife. It works well in mysteries, too.

He was a twenty-year-old kid, a big one. Studying architecture and making money by filming husbands visiting their girlfriend hideaways.

He did not do blackmail. He told me that. He could have, but then he would be a dead Edgar. He told me that too. Like I said, smart kid. He just handed the videos over to the wives and forgot everything. So he was lucky Edgar. Big, lucky Edgar. Being big probably had something to do with the luck.

He had been doing this work eight months. He was a real paid detective, not a bumble-into-it like me. He did what most detectives do—a lot of sleaze. I was a dilettante next to him, but I did crime. I was senior, too, because I had money, not to mention years.

I offered him something slightly above sleaze rates and he jumped. He was free, no classes during holidays. He was mine for a couple of days, ten hours a day.

At school he was learning concrete. During Navidad he was taking a break from study and all the math. An architect needed math. In Mexico he also needed other

155

skills, like how to watch men mixing cement with too much sand and the wrong kind of rocks. He needed to make sure a building would not fall down if it jiggled a little with an everyday earthquake, or a once-and-a-while explosion. Detective work made good architect training.

I liked Edgar. He would be a great Watson to me, but he was not cheap, fifteen dollars a day. That was a lot for me, a man living on social security rates. And to do something special like this, he said he must have an assistant. Five more bucks. I said OK.

I met his assistant right after I met him—Concha, she was his *novia*, his girlfriend. The plan was for them to go to the park in front of Frank's address and then kiss or do whatever, watching for anyone who came out the door. Then take pictures. The opposite of what Edgar normally did at the cheap motels when the guys being watched were the ones with the girls.

The pair looked young and capable and couples kissing from eight <u>AM</u> to midnight were not that unusual. You did it when you could, before work if you needed to. Maybe having the same couple going that long was unusual, but no one checked them out closely. They all looked the same, anyway.

I finished up with Edgar and met with Randy. She and I talked about New Year's—only one more day to go. We were going celebrate it at the Señora's with a real traditional Oaxaca party. I had assumed I was invited, but Randy had gotten a verbal invite from the Señora. Invitations were informal down here once you were in the family. I was in, so they forgot to tell me anything, knowing I would come, but I was still clueless about times. They were the same every year. I just needed to remember the year before. I took my share of mezcal last year, so it was not just old-man leaky memory, the facts were fuzzy to start with. But I was not worried about being late. That was not possible in Mexico. Anyway, Randy knew everything.

Randy had one more day before flying back. I told her I was making headway on her case, the way a real detective would report. She did not ask for more. She did not want to know more, I figured. Her NGO did good for the world, Santo Gordo sometimes did not. And details could be messy, sometimes bloody messy. Too messy for someone in her job. She said they were going to take down the Food for All website when I confirmed it was shady. FfA had a contract, so she had to be careful and wait for me. That was all she told me. I told her I was close.

I shared a little more about Oaxaca Chocolate with her. How we had a bunch of dumb cousins and dead ends. A lot better than dead people, but I figured Efraím would want more. He wanted payback. That was the way a man did things when his place got blown up. The government was hard to touch. They would not pay. Someone needed to. I did not tell Randy about the payback part.

She had met a group of NGO women that day while I had been working near Frank's. They ran a house where young women from villages came when they moved into the big city. It was a nice place she said. Part state, part Catholic, part charity. Randy worked on the charity part, she and her website team. "This group is very transparent. They do good work. They do good."

Good again. It was everywhere.

We two had dinner–more leafy stuff to make Randy happy–and then I went back and thought about sleep, but I was not going to get any for a while. I had thinking to do.

She went out with her new friends from the NGO to do some evening touristing. I stayed back, but she made me promise to go the next day to the rug village, to go rugging, as she called it. I liked the place where they were heading. But it was with three women, the two new friends and Randy. Then I learned it was five. Lupe was coming and baby Beto too.

That explained why I was invited. Someone had to do baby duty. That was OK. I would have Edgar, my new assistant on detective duty. He had become the new professional wing of Santo Gordo, Inc. I would watch Beto. He would watch Frank. His job would be easier, but I would get a break from thugs and crooks. Watching them is like seeing bad movies. Watching babies is like studying monkeys in a cage. More fun.

****

Randy got up early again. Lupe was always up early. Baby Beto too. They came up to my room making noise–I had left the door open–so I was up too and thinking caffeine.

I went down and sat on the stone bench in the courtyard waiting, looking at the fountain, mostly asleep, wondering if Edgar and Concha were on duty yet.

The friends showed up in a cab. Everyone was cheery and festive except baby Beto and me. Beto was asleep; I was not. The women came in a small cab, two of them. Then they wanted three more of us and the baby to squeeze in. That was five plus the driver, not an abnormal load for a cab. The driver did not care. I did. I got old-man cranky.

You need to be friendly when you are shoehorned into a car. The women were already into the fourth level of friendliness. Randy saw to that. I was not even at level one.

Squeezing in was never easy for me and now, when part of me was plastered up with the cast, and I knew I would get the baby in the front. It was too much.

Randy laughed. "I thought they were bringing a van. You stay here. We're going rugging and weaver watching. And meet some rug ladies who have a co-op."

I was relieved. I wanted to be nice, but it takes a while to build up my nice reserves in the morning. Niceness drains out of me when I sleep, like water from a leaky tank, like the one on the roof. But after an espresso or two, a little to eat, a couple of eggs, and a donut, then I have a tank full of nice again. I was not worried.

"Why don't you watch Beto while we are away?" She handed me the baby–I one-armed it–and took a bag from Lupe. Lupe looked surprised but did not get to protest. Me either. I was sleep numb and slow. Beto woke and started laughing.

They gave me formula and extra diapers and a bag bigger than I use when traveling for a week. They hopped in the cab and left.

Randy stuck her head out. "There is a Babysnugger in the bag. You can put it on to carry Beto." They laughed and waved. "See you for comida. Have fun."

Babysnugger.

I stood there. Baby Beto was looking up at me, wiggling his parts. What just happened? Beto was wondering the same.

I held him like a football, cradled in the cast. It made a good cradle, just lumpy.

I thought about breakfast so we two guys headed over to La Avenida. I put Beto on the table next to the menu now advertising "an assortment of breakfast sweets." La Avenida had gone into baked goods after my pastelería had died. They had added English to their menu, too, while I was not looking, getting global. English creeps into a lot of things in Oaxaca. Special K was up there with huevos rancheros. I ignored it and chewed through a pan dulce looking at Beto. Then slugged down a double.

The caffeine kicked in, and I realized my mistake. I had not locked the door that morning. Sometimes when you get old, locking yourself in is the best way. But that was past history, as detectives say when they are on a case. Beto started yelling. I got out a bottle and did the coo-coo-coo with him. He got happy. I tried to.

The Avenida crowd was having fun. No one had ever seen me with anyone before breakfast. No one had ever seen me with a baby. Most days, I growled through my food. They loved my new baby kissing act.

I suspect that needed this training as part of my "degringozation." You had to love babies if you were a real man in Mexico. That was part of the culture. You hugged and kissed and acted like every baby might be your own.

I did my funny face act, the one I did in about the second grade and had not tried since. Baby Beto wiggled on the table while I sipped espresso number two.

They said you could not help loving a baby if you looked long enough. Scientists and mothers said that.

I looked closely at him. He wore some kind of little blue snap-up traveling suit. Randy had brought it. The baby had pale see-through skin, and you could see his skull if you looked closely. To me he looked like some big, half transparent, insect larva wearing clothes, one with blue eyes doing human impersonations. You could not hide his father's north Europe genes.

I looked back at the new menu. Lots of pastries, my real love.

Beto did a yell. I did a quick bottle stuff and all was well. I ate my huevos and Beto sucked the bottle dry. I downed the double. Ideas started firing. My brain engine finally ran full speed.

It was time to catch up with Efraím. I had been doing detective case number two, hunting down Frank, the charity scammer for Randy, and ignoring case one, the bakery blowup. Time to walk over to the cabstand, stretch out my breakfast and plan a little with my cabbie friend.

First I needed to dress. I got out the baby harness, the snugger. It was built for someone with both arms working. It looked like something a steeplejack would wear dangling up a thousand feet, but I got it on, then I got it on right side up. Baby Beto watched. So did the guys at the counter. Santo Gordo was getting closer to sainthood. Or to a comedy act.

We got Beto mounted. It was one of those face-forward things. At least, I hope it was because that was how Baby Beto ended up. He wiggled his fingers and toes and bounced along my belly looking like that creature in the space movie that hatched inside some guy's belly and then popped out, sort of a male birthing. In that movie, the guy died. I was still kicking, like Baby Beto.

We headed down the street, me with my two big arms swinging and he with his two little ones jiggling. I sang a great little choo-choo song, remembered from childhood. Baby Beto gurgled right in time.

The city looks different when you have a baby strapped to your belly. People come up and look. They reach in and touch. Not so much the Oaxacans, they smiled and chatted, but the gringos and especially the gringas, the females. I got oohs and aahs. I got stopped for conversations.

I had built up my "nice" reservoir eating breakfast so I la-la'd along. I learned all about Juana's, the ex-Joann's car problems, I learned about Fawn's dog problems. Mary came by and said that I needed to come visit. She and Joe were having a dinner for friends soon, and please bring the baby, and, oh yes, the mother, too. The baby was a hot topic. The mother was lukewarm. I said maybe.

I got offers and comments no one ever shared when I only had one big old male body.

Then my hair cutter, the Oaxaca lady who lived up the street from me, came up with her girl. She wanted to know all about my daughter Randy and how Beto was doing. He was doing yells so I bounced up and down while we talked. Then Alfonso the butcher came by and asked about Randy, too. I got him to talk about his chickens after a couple of minutes. They were waiting for me anytime, he promised. Randy and Beto were the local gossip theme on my street. I needed to introduce her. They were reminding me.

It was hard to stop the people coming up, but I was on a case, so I moved on.

I got to the cabstand. Efraím had just returned. I could not get in the cab with the belly-extender baby, so I unhooked and went back to my football carry. Beto was almost the right shape, but more rounded, more like a rugby ball than an all-American football. Carrying him felt like an exercise class. I saw why Lupe was in good shape. That and running up and down the stairs hanging clothes and cooking and all the other stuff she did.

I got in and switched to an over-the-shoulder carry. I learned it in Boy Scouts for saving people in a fire. I tried all possibilities for a man with one working arm to carry something live and wiggling, trying to keep Beto quiet as I was talking, "Efraím, what is going on with the bakery?"

He hemmed and hawed. That scared the baby, and he started crying. I did some gentle baby backthumping and there-there-ing and things quieted again.

"Something must be happening. Haven't you talked to your government friends about who put the squeeze on Tío Franciso? Have you checked on the bulldozer? I have tread pictures, evidence I should have told you about. I have clues. For instance, the guy who hired your cousins called from the Llano Park. The clues are yours, but first tell me what is happening. You and your friends must know something."

It took me a mess of confused sentences to say all that. I jumbled the ideas–I was holding the baby flat on my lap playing patty-cake with his feet while I was asking–but Efraím got the idea. I was worrying about the bakery, about what we would do.

"They were not my see-them-everyday family, those two stupid *muchachos*. That was the big and slow part of the family, my cousin and his sons." Efraím was not answering my questions, but he was talking. I did not interrupt. "I put those two to work. They are driving pedicabs out in the village. I bought them used bicycles with back-seat trailers, and they haul fares from the highway bus stop into the main square. I keep them busy with hard work, not like prison, but watched."

He was talking family, not about the government connections, not about the bulldozer, the things I asked about. I figured someone in the government knew Oaxaca Chocolate and its money. Especially the money.

The bakery case seemed to be settling down with no major injuries–if you do not count me and Francisco and the bakery–no shootouts or revenge beatings, so I was hoping it would fade away. But it was Navidad and things were always slow then. They pick up when the new year starts. I tried not to worry.

Efraím was a bit too cagey about the government. I did not want him to take on the rich guys up north. The money from the north could bury Efraím, with a little help from the local government.

The local gringo, the one who paid off the spikehairs, could be a problem too if Efraím went after him too. The government does not like politics and crime to spill over on us visitors from the North. I was not worried because of any allegiance to a fellow American. I was worried because it could do in Efraím. And maybe me, too, now that I think of it.

"Have you started working on the chocolate company?" Efraím asked, reminding me of our deal. I was supposed to scare the guys in the States into forgetting Oaxaca.

"I have someone working on it." It was not quite a lie. Randy would check for me. I figured that before long I would go up there and lead a march around headquarters. Maybe do a press conference about how they screwed the bakery. That would slow them down in the new politically correct consumer world.

I would ask Randy for advice on that. She had been an expert in this type of thing in her youth. Probably still was.

I told Efraím my idea.

"Just blockade the street like we do."

"That does not work in the States. They bring out rubber bullet guns and tear gas and armored buses to haul you away."

"And you freedom lovers let them get away with it?"

Efraím had lived there. He knew. But he liked to taunt me with our all-American freedoms.

"At least in the US we can drive down the street without having to wait out a five-hour blockade by teachers or farmers or anyone who has a complaint." I was defending my homeland. Efraím had pushed a button when he got to blockades. "You and the taxis even blockaded the streets a couple times."

"But we used our own cars to do it. We did not steal buses like the others do."

Efraím had hijacked this conversation. I aimed it back towards the bakery. "So you have some contacts in the government?"

He finally started talking about the government. He did not like to tell me too much, afraid I would talk either with a couple of shots of mezcal or a little police prodding. But this time he opened up. He only did that when he was worried.

"The word to harass the bakery came down from somewhere in Mexico City. No one local here knew why. Oaxaca officials did not know about the chocolate company wanting to buy property; otherwise they would have bought out my Uncle and sold to the Mexico City guys and made a killing. Our local people only had the word to do some harassing. The bulldozer was the same. Word came down from someone in Mexico City to a contractor working nearby on a government project. He went where they said."

That was government as usual. Everyone local will point north when they explain the bad stuff they do, even if they planned it sitting in the Zócalo, two blocks away, next to the Cathedral, and having a beer.

Everyone knew you could not do anything to the government guys. The government took care of its own. The rich Oaxaca Chocolate guys in the States were hard to get at, too. That was my job, anyway. Efraím's cousin's kids, the ones who did the explosion, were now part of Efraím's family. The Mexican messenger who did the payoff that I witnessed had disappeared, I hoped to some other city and not to the next world. The bulldozer guy was just a pawn. That left the gringo connection, the one here in Oaxaca, to pay for everything, pay with a couple hundred pounds of flesh if he was unlucky.

I needed to play my Saint card to keep that gringo out of trouble. Or at least with minor injuries. Best was undiscovered. Problems went away if you buried them deep enough.

No one knew the gringo. Maybe this whole thing could get cleaned up. Like the dirty diaper I was smelling.

The baby yelled, I put the conversation on pause. "I need to do a change." Efraím already knew. I walked over to a bench and rummaged through the bag. It had wipe-this pads and wipe-that cleaner. I did it like a pro.

I had done this sort of thing before. A time or two when Randy was about this size. But never one-handed. Luckily the new diapers made it easy with some tape to hold everything together, not safety pins. Some things stay with you forever, like riding a bicycle or greasing your car. You never forget how and wash up well afterwards.

We were all happy then. Baby Beto smiled, Efraím plotted to find out more, and I thought I could keep things clean, simple, and undiscovered. Stupid me.

I did a goodbye taxista knuckle bump with Efraím. I was getting good at it. Baby Beto did a two-finger shake. He still had some learning to do. Efraím hopped into his cab. A fare was yelling on the radio. That was how he usually escaped.

I kept thinking about what Efraím had said, "What are you going to do to stop the money coming down from Oaxaca Chocolate?" As long as it was flowing, things would be messy. Maybe they still wanted the bakery. But he said it had slowed down. I was hoping it was not just the holidays, but maybe the money spigot was turned off.

I walked back to the Zócalo with my baby belly strapped back on. Benches had cleared out when we got there, so we two guys took a seat, me leaning back, Beto strapped in. He looked like a marionette with a drug-crazed puppeteer pulling strings, wiggling parts. He was trying out his new brain wiring, trying to get his circuits under control. I let my circuits rest.

The time with Efraím had worn them out. I zeroed and looked around like one of the tourists.

The Zócalo was decked out for the holidays. No separation of church and state in Oaxaca. The big nativity scene stood in front of us, with its sheet metal shepherds and sheep. José and María were there too. Sheet metal cuts you even better than glass. I learned that last year.

The main thing you noticed were the *Noche Buena* plants, the poinsettias. Thousands of them grew from green pots stuck deep in soil around the trees, almost buried in the gardens in the square.

Street vendors were swarming over all the walkways.

Every so often, the government tried to throw out these venders, the *ambulantes*, the guys who walked back and forth selling everything from shawls to marimba lessons. Stores wanted to keep all the tourist action, but the *ambulantes* kept coming back. They had to sell to eat. Some, however, were always there—they had made a deal. A cop or official had a percentage of their pesos, I was sure.

Others only showed up on special days. That day was one of them. The unionized teachers were holding a camp-in demonstration on one side of the Zócalo, making speeches, mostly drowned out by musicians playing everything from trombones to Peru flutes.

When the teachers were there, the Zócalo was a free for all. Police stayed back. Street sellers could sit down for a change, laying out their purses, hats, knitted things, blouses, stuffed toys, jewelry, belts, sandals and pirated CDs on sheets of plastic so tourists had to walk through them. Tourists loved these ad hoc labyrinth bazaars. Officials did not. Nothing in it for them.

Beto and I started walking. I was looking. Beto was sleepy, lolling his head like a two-foot bobble-head. Put on a baseball cap and you could sit him up on any dashboard.

I had never attracted clowns in the Zócalo before. They came that day. I hired one to keep Beto happy. The clown twisted a four-balloon wiener dog. It popped. That led to a ten-minute cry.

I had done a half dozen Christmases in Oaxaca, and the show was fun but not as exciting to me as for newcomers. And it was crowded. I had enough trouble fitting through the crowd when I was just me. That day with Baby Beto, I felt like the elephant in a china shop.

The day was slipping by, and I wanted to see how Edgar and Concha were "surveilling," a word I never heard until I was 50. I had read it in the news. I liked it. A good detective word.

I walked a couple of blocks. I could not dawdle. Babies want you to keep moving–it reminds them of better times when they were back in their mommie womb, a lot better than a Babysnuggie.

We reached the little plaza. My junior detectives were going at it. Maybe more than I paid them for. I was wondering if they would notice anything, even me, but Concha broke the lip-hold and popped up. She came over and goo-gooed the baby.

She had more to say than the goo-goo. "This is not going to work. My lips are wearing out. They were not made for ten hours a day of this."

"You could just talk and look into each other's eyes. Maybe cry a little. Edgar could cry too. You don't need to kiss all the time."

"Tell that to Edgar. He said he had instructions, and they were go at it."

I got the problem settled. And found that our bad guy Frank had not come out the door that day.

It was the day before New Year's, and people were traveling. I probably should have saved money and waited until the next week, but I did want to settle this before Randy went back.

I left my two lusty Watsons on their bench, doing sad-eyed, love looks. I hoped they were acting. I had brought them a lip glosser. I should have bought more protection. I figured they would end up needing it. I did not want another baby named after me

****

I went back home. The women had gotten back, too. I exchanged Baby Beto for Randy. The exchange went well, and we two left to eat. She was hungry after her rugging. I was just hungry.

I took her to the Moroccan place. She wanted to do floor sitting at the low metal table. I told her she could yell over to me. I was going to sit at a regular table, one my legs would go under.

"I do not do yoga. I stretch my money, not my body parts."

She gave me that you-are-such-an-old-pain-in-the-ass look but came over and we ordered. It was lamb day. I did the carnivore. She did falafel and tabouli.

Randy also did her inner anthropologist with the owner and found out all about her. I listened and drank a cerveza waiting for the food. Her son had gone to Canada to work, got a job in a Moroccan restaurant, learned secret recipes, and finally came back. Canada was their Moroccan connection. You learn more than hamburgers and fries when you go north these days. Globalization was everywhere.

My lamb arrived—meat chunks, lying still for their afternoon siesta on a heap of couscous. I prodded them, woke them a little with my fork. They agreed it was time for eating and jumped into my mouth. We would take our naps together later.

We talked. I mean Randy quizzed. I did a full dump of all the news about the bakery, about the cousins and their newfound bicycle taxis, about Tío Francisco saving everyone when the gas leaked, about me and my hard head saving the building from the bulldozer, about Oaxaca Chocolate causing it all. She was impressed. I did not tell her I was afraid of what Efraím was going to do.

"You put your head on the line for your friend. I am starting to believe you are an all right guy." She had not believed it years ago when I worked for the coal company and she marched in demonstrations wearing a gas mask in front of my office window. But now we were on the same side. More or less.

"Let me check on the Oaxaca Chocolate Company. You know I have some connections." I had hoped she would say that.

I went back home and did my nap. She hit the streets in mad-dog Englishman, sunstroke mode. Then it was evening. Church bells rang. Birds flew up from the church roof. Sun shadows grew long enough to hide in, and I went out. For my wakeup walk around the block.

Carlos was there. Sitting on the bench. He came over and we did some old man word jousting like old men are supposed to.

"Heard you and a baby were on the streets." Everyone knew everything.

"Randy, my daughter, is in town." I left him to puzzle out what that meant about the baby.

"You know I've been thinking about your book. The one when you become a saint—we will need pictures, so don't lose any weight" He laughed his best horselaugh. "I'm talking up the book online already. I think I have some nibbles." He paused for a second and looked at me, like a priest would if he were going to set me straight on some fine point in theology. "With you being a saint, maybe we can do holy tours for tourists here Oaxaca?"

Nothing he said was worth answering that day.

"I have an appointment with the kid from the pueblo," he said after a long dry wait for me to respond.

Carlos shook hands and walked off. He looked happy. More than meeting me should merit. We all knew about the kid dropping off his baggie every week, Oaxaca's version of the delivery man, like the one who used to come around in Baltimore when I was young, but this one dropped off *mota*–marijuana, not milk. That kept Carlos happy. It kept a lot of expats happy. I was happy with my churros and mezcal. But I could get happier sometimes.

I thought about my two mysteries as I resumed walking around the park, doing slow laps as my after-nap exercise.

Two mysteries were almost too much for a nap-muddled brain to handle. I kept getting details mixed up. First the mystery about the gringo, the local connection who paid for the bakery to blow–the connection Efraím wanted to find and the one I wanted Efraím to forget. Then, the second mystery, this guy Frank with the charity scam that Randy was after–the one Edgar was snooping out.

What would I do with Frank when I found him, anyway? Edgar would follow him when he came out. I just wanted the Frank guy to go away, but I promised Randy I would do something. Efraím would know what to do.

Frank did not sound like your average expat. Average was retired or dropped by some company for a younger guy. Average was someone who had worked his butt off and now was tired, straw-hatting it in the sun and if lucky, getting his Social Security or if not, praying the government would not snatch it away before he got there. A little left politically–but not far, a little low financially–maybe pretty far, a little high sometimes-who knew how far, and always right-on, sitting on the balcony looking out over the city sipping at something with a friend or two.

This scam guy sounded more like your basic grifter. Probably hiding out from his past in the States. The noir kind I read about in mysteries, saw movies about, but never met. I was not sure how I would scare him off. He scared me. He always carried a little gun in the movies. Or at least a long, skinny knife. The kind that go in deep.

Those thoughts took me a couple of laps around the park. I had thought enough for one day. I took a rest on a bench. The kids at the school at the end of the park were warming up their drum and bugle brigade. Twenty boys and girls attacked their drums. The same number played random notes on bugles. They all stamped their feet. Then the teacher came and they got louder. A rocket or two went off and they started down the street with a melody under all the extra notes. It was New Year's Eve. Time to head home.

Año Nuevo

I sat there waiting. Randy had gone to mass with Lupe and María and the Señora. The men were off someplace. The children were playing. They put me in the front room next to the TV and played a DVD for me, Bart Simpson Christmas again.

I tried not to be annoyed but I wanted to think about what was coming up, the food. I turned the TV off and the Señora's son came in to see how I was doing. He had been in the garden talking with friends. The men were planning something. Some getaway. Probably to go see one holy virgin or another at a shrine. That was what you did for kicks in Mexico. Or went to the beach. Or maybe a package deal with both.

Finally the family assembled in the courtyard. The food came out to greet us too. Not my normal feast food *mole*, but instead, pork, a roast that had been soaked for a day in cider–the getting-drunk kind with alcohol. Then the roast got more cider–they injected it when the guy was baking, lying there sweating, surrounded by garlic and onions and all the Mexican herbs, along with almonds and raisins to sweeten its piggy temperament.

God, I loved eating here. María and her stove were straight from heaven. I guess I have to give the Señora credit too. She was the boss for this place.

The roast was served with *ensalada rusa*, Russian salad. No one was sure why it was Russian. Potatoes started out in the New World, not the old and the Russians do not make salad from potatoes, they drink them.

Mexicans enrich the normal American version. Sure they have potatoes and peas and carrots, but instead of just mayonnaise to goop it all together, the people here do one part mayonnaise to two parts cream.

For this meal there was no fooling around. We ate meat. We ate a cholesterol-loaded salad. That was it. And we drank. The Señora served the same cider that the pig bathed in. We felt one with the pork. What a meal.

I finished one serving and then my cell rang.

It took a while to find the phone in my pants pockets. By that time the so-called ringing had gone on a while. My ringtone, the Star Spangled Banner, played–a friend at the phone store's joke. I did not know how to change the thing. But it did not ring often.

Edgar started talking. "He left his apartment. He must be the one. He looks skinny and has a tee shirt and jeans. He is old."

By that I was sure he meant at least in his thirties.

"I have taken several pictures. I will bring them to you tomorrow. How do you want them big or little?"

"Big. And good work. Do you know him?"

"I have not seen him before, but I do not go to the tourist areas often where the Americans stay. He is one of you from above the border."

I had assumed he was American. I was right.

"I followed him, but I must go home now. I sent Concha already. I do not want her in this part of town."

"Where are you? What is he doing?"

"He is in the area of prostitution. On Zaragoza."

It sounded like a polite report on an errant husband to the wife. Edgar used formal terminology.

I had seen the area with its parade of crotch-high skirts and low-drooped tops. Women were chunky and a lot of flesh showed. I guessed our charity scammer Frank was celebrating New Year's Eve in his own way. But then, maybe he celebrated that way every night.

"Please, go home Edgar. Thank you. We can talk tomorrow. You did well."

He had a picture of the guy. Now I needed to make sure Frank really was Mister Food for All and then decide what to do with him. Going to the police would be stupid and could mess up Randy's charity work. I would talk to Efraím.

I went back to my pork. Lupe brought me serving two. The roast had waited without complaint, keeping warm and happy. I quit thinking about Edgar and went back into eating gear, trying for a slow one. This was too good to chomp through. I looked around and saw I was eating alone. Everyone else had finished and talking.

Randy kept explaining how things were to the Señora. How Lupe and Beto were going to be well off, independent. Lupe was silent. She was supposed to move out. That was what Randy said.

At first I was worried the Señora would not survive this. She did not take well to any new authority in her neighborhood. She had chased a priest out of town, the one who said Mexicans prayed too much to Mary and not enough to Jesus. She had feuded with the lady down the street over the Virgin's clothes. She kept her son in line and ruled the house. She would bide her time and have everything back under control when Randy went home. I was sure.

I finished just in time, almost midnight–time for grapes. I never understood how eating one grape at each chime of the clock connected to a good year coming up, but everyone believed it. Like with the Immaculate Conception or the tooth fairy, believing was the important part. Believing together made you part of the community. So I tried. But the tooth fairy was easier to believe in.

I had not been able to master the grape-a-second throw-down in the past. I usually made it up to eight or so before I got behind the clock.

Bong. It started with the Señora's clock on the mantle. She always kept it fast, ahead of the church and the fireworks. In the Señora's house you lived on her time, so I started with grape one. Easy.

Then grape two. Not hard. But at six I was suffering mouth clog.

I did seven, missed eight, and started to grab for water. But pride won out, and I went on to nine and ten. That was the killer. Almost.

It lodged somewhere half way down the wrong pipe. And stayed there. I tried to gag it out. The grape did not move. I tried to cough it up. Nothing. Then the edges of the room got grey and zoomed in like the finish of some old black and white movie.

"Santo Gordo humbled by a grape." My final thought was getting fuzzy when arms grabbed me and squeezed hard. The grape shot out and hit the wall next to the picture of Jesus hanging above the flowers. I dropped in a chair.

Life came back. The Señora crossed herself. The lights in my head came on, and I looked up at Jesus and the grape stain on the wall. A new year, truly, was coming for me. One that almost did not make it.

Everyone laughed. A nervous laugh. I turned and saw it was Randy who had me. She patted me on the shoulder. My near death stopped time for a couple of seconds. Then it came back to me. Edgar found him, found Frank. I would have to deal with that in the new year. And Oaxaca Chocolate too.

"*Feliz Año Nuevo*, Happy New Year," we yelled. Well, they did. I stayed sitting and sipped at a glass of water, thinking the new year sounded a lot like the old one.

****

I did not have to worry about my normal New Year's Day hangover. I went to sleep much too sober right after my grape attack. When I woke, my ribs were sore where Randy saved me, but my head was clear.

Randy was leaving. Her four days in Oaxaca were over. She was downstairs, dragging her suitcase, hugging the family and squeezing the baby. I joined in and watched out for the cab. The Señora was there hugging and kissing. Lupe and María, too. No one in the house was sleeping. They all came to say goodbye.

"New Year's Day is a good day to fly," Randy explained. "The planes aren't full. I read that the crowd returning to the States doesn't start for another day or two."

She was analytic and probably right. Most visitors were smart and still asleep in some relative's bed or in the hotel, not like us at seven AM.

But I had to be my old man self and argue a little. "You can be sure the most junior pilot is flying your plane. Anyone with pull is with their family. And your pilot probably stayed up half the night."

"That's why they have autopilots," Randy countered. She did not worry. She was still young and thought life was something doable. I hoped she stayed that way.

The cab pulled up. The driver knew me. I shook his hand. He loaded the bags, and Randy and I took the back seat.

I started in on my update.

181

"I need to tell you what I found. I think I found the guy with the charity. He looks like a sleaze. But I'll question him to make sure. Maybe today."

"What do you mean by sleaze?"

"Drugs, loose-change women, you know."

Randy rolled her eyes. I could not say whore in front of my girl yet, and prostitute sounded too formal.

"Thanks, Dad. But say prostitute. I know about them. I even know them. Help them. Sex workers is the way to say it these days. Remember that."

I filed the word under new-speak in my head in case it came up again, and went back to my detective briefing. "That doesn't prove he ran the scam, but he doesn't seem like your normal expat, or at least the kind I know. He's in a cheap room by the old railroad tracks. I'll call you soon." That set a target for me. A nice soft one.

Randy hugged me, like I had done something good. I guess I had. I felt like I was doing it for Oaxaca too.

"What about your bakery mystery? The one you and your friend are in."

"It's developing. Nothing happened during the holidays."

"You mean nothing but almost getting yourself killed."

A lot of people almost got killed, but that does not count for detectives. Randy was looking worried, like a parent does when her kid is out after curfew.

"I probably will have to come to San Francisco. Maybe soon." This was a big surprise. I should have told her earlier. "I have to do something about this Oaxaca

Chocolate Company, up there. Want to help me picket the place?"

She started laughing, probably remembering how red-faced angry I got when she went picketing and how lock-the-girl-up mad when she targeted my company, back when she was young and I thought work was something I would do forever. Work dropped me early for some cheap college grad, and I ended up here. Randy still was picketing. Some things do not change, some do.

"Well, come see me. We can go touristing in the city after picketing. You can stay with me. I only have a studio but the sofa with the dog is always free."

Being old lets you dodge some things, like sofas. And dogs are not good bedmates. I was thinking cheap hotel but smiled and kept quiet.

I went on about how nice it was to see her. She went on thanking me for my help. We were tight. Like some sitcom of the '50s. No fights, no differences of opinion, no nothing. But goodbye fluff was ok. They say that no one wants to read stories when there is no conflict, but it sure makes life better.

The cab was leaving the city limits, nearing the airport. The Walmart was closed. Everything was closed. Even the pizza and chicken stands were closed.

The airport was empty like the highway.

She got out and took the bags. I started to go inside, but she pushed me back.

"You go back and rest. You'll mess up your old-man routine if you get up too early." I let her persuade me.

She pecked me with another daughter kiss. I did the hug. It was a soap opera ending. And she went in.

The driver was looking forward to the empty road on the way back, so I told him to take off. We did fifty. The car and I bounced over the holes. The taxista could not resist racing up the open highway even if it shook his cab and passenger into pieces.

We got to the Zócalo in ten minutes. I jumped out and aimed for an outdoor restaurant, grabbing a table near the espresso machine. The Zócalo was always open because some tourists are crazy and might get up early any day. But there were no street vendors yet. Just yawning waiters in black ties and white shirts. And me.

****

I sat there in the Zócalo thinking, finishing off my espresso.

I had to file the bakery away for a while and work on Randy's problem. I needed to talk with Efraím about Frank, the guy my junior detective had followed, about what to do. But first, I still had no real confirmation he was the Food for All guy. The evidence was circumstantial–that was what they called it on TV. I needed a smoking gun. Or at least a hot donation. But first I wanted to check in with Edgar.

He would still be watching. I walked back down to the little plaza.

Edgar was there. Alone.

"Concha would not come this morning. She slept in. So I brought my broom and was sweeping up, looking like I cleaned around the church." This guy was a natural. He would make detective first class quick. Edgar handed me a photo.

I took it and then gave Edgar a handshake. "I want to thank you. You found him."

"Just pay me. That is enough."

He stopped speaking and looked over at the gate. I turned too. Frank walked out. I did not need to see the photo, I saw the real thing, a low life living it up–well, at least living. Someone that looked like a crook. Perfect casting. It made me a little suspicious.

Edgar smiled and picked up his bag, the one with the camera. He handed me his broom and turned to follow Frank, who had reached the corner.

Frank never noticed anything. He was in a hurry, walking down towards the railroad. Something was happening, and Edgar was like a dog with a detective itch. I managed to tell Edgar before he got far, "Call me if he comes back this way."

I had an idea.

I sat looking at the trees. I counted to a hundred four times. Four hundred was enough.

I walked casually, as casually as any American could in this neighborhood, along the wall to Frank's gate. It was closed, but anything would open the old catch. I jimmied it with a credit card. I had watched guys do it in movies lots of times. It worked.

The place inside was quiet. I figured anyone there would be asleep that day. Edgar said Frank was the only one who came out. Maybe no one else lived there. I did not know. I was quiet.

I stood in a narrow courtyard between two buildings. The buildings stood tall enough and close enough to keep out direct light, actually most light, but it was bright enough for me to see that windows for the rooms were closed, with newspapers hung across them. Stuff piled in the courtyard made it hard to get to most of the rooms. I figured they were vacant. Only one room looked completely free of trash blockades in front of the door. This must be it, Frank's place. You could see where someone had been through the walk recently. It had to be Frank's.

I did not try the door. I was not that brave. I looked at the windows with their rows of horizontal slats of glass, stacked one above the other, each two inches high, built so you could crank the panes to angle them and let air in. You could also reach in between the slats with the coat hanger I had picked up. It was the least dirty thing I had seen lying around. I wiggled it in the space between the glass slats and caught the curtain. I slid it back. Just a little. No one yelled. That was good sign.

I saw a small bed and a desk with a chair. A suitcase was half under the unmade bed. Nothing more. A light bulb hung down from a wire in the ceiling. No doorways inside for a closet, no bath, not even a sink. The toilet must be off the courtyard in the back. I changed my mind about this guy living it up. He was barely living.

I pulled the curtain to the edge of the window, and more light got in. The desk was flimsy. The chair, too. It would not hold anyone big.

I heard a noise and let go of the curtain. Some animal had jumped in the back. I jumped too, cut my last remaining good hand on the window and started sucking blood. I did not want to leave any on the curtains.

I wrapped my hand in my shirttail. It did not hurt much and had not dripped much. That encouraged me to look again, not run.

On the desk, I saw it. I wanted to take a picture. But I did not need any evidence. I was not going to court. I was going to Randy. She would believe me. It was her logo—FfA. On a sheet of paper with some writing on it.

Frank had to be the one. No one else lived here. FfA did.

I put the curtain back with my damaged hand. Then the Star Spangled Banner played in my pocket.

No one looked out. More proof no one was here. Frank really was the only one. I held the phone up to my ear.

"He went up to the carwash. He bought something and is heading back. We are almost there."

Carwashes were our local drug distribution centers. You name it they had it. Most people went in a car for the pickup. Frank just walked, no car, no nothing. He had proved that drugs could eat your whole paycheck, or all your donations.

I got out quick and went to the church a block away, standing like I was waiting for a mass. Churches have masses all the time in Oaxaca. I figured one would be coming soon, like a bus. Waiting was fine but a half hour later, mass started, so I ducked out the side and called Edgar. He was back on his post watching the door. I told him come meet me for breakfast up in the Zócalo.

****

"I am calling it off."

"But you said a week. You get a week from me. That is how it works."

"I do not need a week. We nailed Frank." I did not tell Edgar what I found or why I was interested in this guy. I just said it was over. "You must have other things to do. The holidays are full of events and weddings and parties. Concha needs to be taken out someplace. Go do it."

"You told me that you would pay for a week and I believed you. I turned down a wonderful opportunity to follow a bus driver. His wife thinks he makes unauthorized stops. But after I said no to her job, she left him to stay at her sister's. I gave up that offer to work for you."

I was not sure if he was telling the exact truth, but I would pay for his week, anyway. I might need Edgar in the future, maybe this week if something happened on the bakery case. I wanted to keep him happy. I had the pesos. During my posada week, lying unconscious and mostly dead I saved a lot of money.

"Hello, Concha, I will see you in ten minutes." Edgar wasted no time with his new freedom. "I have a bundle of money from the boss, and I am ready to go."

He pulled the cell away from his ear looking at it like he did not believe what it was saying.

"Concha, get up, you can sleep when you are old, like Señor Gordo, not now when you are young and your *novio* is rich." Edgar was the only person in town happy to be awake before noon that day.

I told Edgar he was on call. I might phone him sometime during the week. He said that the cell does not work well all the time—keep trying.

It did not work well at the beach with Concha. That was my guess.

I took off. I was sure Efraím was on duty by then. I walked the five blocks to his stand.

Detective work was going to make me into *Santo Flaco*, Saint Skinny. Recently I had walked more than any pilgrim, but I was feeling good. One case was solved. I felt like I had won something. Of course, Frank was still running around. But Efraím would know what to do to slow him down.

****

Efraím was in the cab.

"Let's get a coffee," I yelled to him, pointing at the coffee shop nearby.

He jumped out. Ephraim was either getting mellowed or getting rich. He was stepping out of his cab more and more. I hoped it was mellowing. The second was OK, but getting rich meant making connections and probably not good ones.

I ordered my espresso and did a cheesecake slice. They were everywhere now, like the gringos who ate them. Ephraim had his usual for this time of day, a lemonade.

"I have news."

"You found Oaxaca Chocolate?

"No, not that news. Something else." I wanted to boast about solving the hopped up, scam-grabbing, low-life Frank case. And get some help on what to do next. Efraim wanted to talk chocolate.

"I think it is time for you to go up there and talk to those chocolate people before something else happens with their money down here. Make sure they forget my uncle's building."

"I have to wait until the holidays are over. No one is anywhere until then. Even in the States."

Navidad holidays in Mexico last until the Three Wise Men show up a week into the new year. That is when traditional kids get their present. But times are changing. Coca Cola is subverting the three visitors, using Santa and his bag of tricks and toys. It will probably work. Kids love the fat guy. Then everyone can forget the Wise Men and get back to work early, like us gringos up north.

In the States, you have already been back at work a week before the three show up. Santa comes down the chimney, then the new year ball drops and Bam! Holidays are over.

No easing back to work while you wait for the wise guys from the East to say hi. But I did not tell Efraím that holidays were over in the US. I wanted to wait a little before my trip.

"I am looking for a ticket, but I need some help on something else. Something new. Something for Randy." I explained my triumphant investigation. "Now, I just want this guy to go away."

I had said it the wrong way, the way a mafia don talks just before he gets some guy whacked. I only wanted Frank to fade out.

"What should I do?" I asked again.

Ephraim was not in a good mood for dealing with problem gringos. I should have waited. He asked, "Why do you care?"

"He got Randy involved."

"OK, then we will fix it. Leave it to me."

I tried to explain more, but Efraím said he had to run. He was working on getting the bakery rebuilt. He turned and got in the cab.

"Where is this guy? What is his name?" He called back over his shoulder

I told him the address and walked up handing over the photo.

"Don't hurt him."

Efraím smiled big. "I would not hurt a fly."

I was not thrilled with his reply. I had seen Efrain grab flies from the air and throw then down so hard they popped.

Sometimes you start things rolling, and you have to trust they go the right direction. That was what I had always done with Efraím and he with me. We had managed to stay alive through those times. A couple of other people did not.

Then Ephraim and his cab were gone.

I looked down. The cheesecake looked up. It wondered why it was still there. I finished it off, not thinking of Efraím or Frank even once. I was getting good at conscience cleaning. I was always good at plate cleaning.

****

I finished off New Year's Day sleeping.

I got up late, snacked a little, and telephoned Randy.

She had been in San Francisco for a couple of hours. Her flight back was easy. The ride to her apartment, too. She was cooking.

"Here's the news. I saw the FfA documents in this guy Frank's room. He used to be at the address you gave me. He moved. There was nothing to make me think he had any kind of charity. Except one for himself. And for the drugs we saw him buying."

"He's gone tonight." I figured she meant from her website. "And thanks, I knew you could put on your detective suit, your Santo Gordo suit, and figure this out."

Case closed, but I would make more sure with Efraím's help. No need to tell Randy about that.

"And I'll check on that company for you, Oaxaca Chocolate. There has to be something on it, even if you didn't find it on the web. Don't worry."

I figured she would find something. She seemed pretty well connected up there. Then I would head up and see what was happening.

"Now you get some rest." She did a quick goodbye and hung up. That lady was all business when she was at home. She should vacation more.

After the call, my week dawdled by. I dawdled, too. Randy was gone. Efraím was busy. I lazed on the terrace sipping iced tea in the afternoon and mezcal at night.

Early January was waiting time. Kids waited for the Three Kings to show. Tourists waited for their flight home. Even the sun seemed to be waiting until the last minute to come up.

I did not wait. I started living my old life again right away. Doing nothing important.

I took espresso first thing and did my morning walk. I ate a man-sized comida and returned for siesta. I did late afternoon on the terrace. I said hello to my friends and neighbors. I even cleaned up my place. Clothes and dishes had stacked up while I recuperated and did my daddy bit with Randy along with my Santo Gordo crime-stopper two-step. It was the time to let sleeping crimes lie.

Life slowed. I did, too. We were a good match.

I forgot those healthy green leaves and shoots that sprouted up whenever Randy chose from the menu. I ate traditional, real food. I ate real fatty, real cheesy, real meaty and really spiced. My stomach and I were old-fashioned that way.

I did one buffet, my quota per week. I went early and stayed until they pushed me out the door. I did the best one, the one near the cathedral, the traditional one, with *mole negro*, of course, but with ribs in red sauce and pork backbone in green sauce and beef brisket in yellow sauce. And soups to wash everything down. They only needed hammocks for taking a siesta, and it would have been heaven.

I did this for five faultless days. Nights were different, though. I woke up dreaming of Frank. I woke up seeing a big knife cutting a limp hose. I woke up dreaming of chocolate pouring down from el Norte. And worst of all, I woke up with concrete falling on my head.

I wanted to end it all, the loose ends that is. Only Santo Gordo could do that. So I called Efraím.

"I am working on it. Tonight we go visit with your friend Frank."

****

It was after eight when Efraím called that night. He simply said, "Time to go."

I walked down the stairs and went through the courtyard, wondering if I really should do this. I had talked Efraím into letting me go along, to watch. I thought things would not get out of control if I were there. I could not

194

stop anything, but Efraím would think twice with me sitting in the front.

I was surprised at how angry Efraím had gotten.

Everyone knows Mexico is full of criminals—or at least full of crimes. Crimes were everywhere, but criminals were harder to locate. Big ones got away, and small ones got protected. Not like the States where the big ones also slipped away, but little ones were hauled in while the big crooks cheered the police on.

When Efraím had found out Frank was from the States, he exploded. He wanted to make Randy's charity chiseler pay for all the crimes of the chocolate company, the oil companies, the gold companies and everyone from the States who had ever done wrong to Mexico, for all Frank and my country's sins. I just wanted to keep things from escalating.

The street was dark with no cabs when I went out after Efraím's call. Two headlights at the corner flashed. I walked towards them and an oversized SUV, one of the long, black ones, the kind that government officials and secret cops used, pulled beside me. They say drug gangs used them too. No plates, no ID, driving with headlights turned off—that meant a big shot from one side or the other owned the thing. Its fancy chrome wheels said it was very special. They were big enough to ford rivers or run down little Nissans and Volkswagens.

What I noticed most were the windows—dull black, with a soft glow floating in them, like boulder-sized gemstones cut to fit the window openings. Gems any devil would love to wear around his neck.

I saw nothing inside the car, only black.

The back door sprung open and one of the brothers jumped out, the ones who blew up the bakery and who now—Efraím assured me—were on our side.

"I am Ricardo." He came to shake my hand but Efraím yelled, "Get in, Santo. Rudolfo and Ricardo are helping. We will have formal introductions at my house someday. This is not a party."

Ricardo opened the front door for me and handed me a plastic bag full of clothes.

I decided to stay silent. Efraím stared straight ahead and motioned for me to buckle up. I figured that meant fast driving was coming. Seatbelts are for looks in Mexico, unless you are racing or a tourist.

"Just in case," he said.

The two young men in the back were silent, too. Efraím must have already explained everything. Or they were afraid to talk. I opened the bag. I pulled out a black suit coat, a tie, and gloves, black leather ones.

"Put them on. We are un-Americanizing your looks. You have three problems. You are pink, have a broken arm and a round shape everyone knows. So we cover you, like some Spanish lady going to church in disguise. Put on the coat and tie but wait for the *pasamontañas*."

I did not know that meant, but when I reached in the bag again and felt around, I found something, a ski mask, the kind some bank robber would wear if he wanted to look stylish.

I got the coat on. It was a big one—God knows where Efraím found one this size. It fit right over the cast.

"Button your coat. Any Oaxacan would always keep it buttoned. And pull the tie tight. Don't look sloppy, like you normally do."

I was not sloppy. I was almost Mexican, I thought. But I kept quiet and followed orders. Efraím was running this show, and he was tense. My job that night was to cool things down. I could debate him later.

I could have gone naked or worn a clown suit, and no one outside the car would have known. The windows were dark enough to hide everything. But these clothes were for Frank to see when we picked him up, not for the outside world.

I finished dressing and looked like a cheap thug. Just right. I squeezed into the gloves. Maybe I looked Mexican, but I looked like a big one. I guess that was good for what we were planning.

After five minutes, my eyes adjusted to the dark windows. I could see out. No one that we passed tried to look in. They all looked the other way. No one wanted to see anything. They acted like the car was invisible–a good idea when secret cops or gang goons were in your neighborhood. Whistle and look someplace else. That was our American way, too. I knew that from my kid days in Baltimore and my years working.

We drove fifteen minutes. Efraím was talking on the radio to some taxistas watching Frank. We neared the railroad tracks, not my favorite place, but a perfect one for a kidnapping. We put on ski masks. I got the three holes right after a couple tries and could finally see and breathe at the same time.

Frank was walking in front of us. He speeded up, loping almost, as the car slowed down behind him. Efraím edged the car beside him, and Ricardo jumped out while we moved. Rodolfo did the same from the other side, and they grabbed Frank's arms and slid him in the back seat. He rolled across and tried to jump out.

This always looked simple in the movies. Frank almost got away. Rudolfo ran around and pushed him back. Frank started crying.

Efraím said two words, "Search him." Ricardo and Rodolfo went at it better than the airport guys in New York City. They found knives, one small, one big enough to kill you, a wallet, and some cigarettes. They stuck the cigarettes back in his pocket. That quieted him a little.

I watched in the mirror, sitting quiet as Efraím had told me.

Efraím drove 80 miles an hour and everything outside got out of our way—cabs, buses, people, and police. Nothing wanted to be involved with a no-plates, lights-off, black SUV. We passed the airport in five minutes and reached the country where the roadsides were almost empty.

Everyone in the car stayed quiet. Frank, too. He looked down and held his head in his hands. The two backseat R-boys, Ricardo and Rudolfo, held him by the arms. They looked like black skulls for the Day of the Dead, with the outlines of white eyes and glowing painted teeth painted on their masks. The boys would grunt every once in a while like some animal getting ready to gnaw at something. Frank shut his eyes and trembled a little.

Efraím started quietly, "We do not like gringos coming down here to steal. That is our job. It makes us very unhappy."

We hit one of the street bumps made to slow the passing cars. We all flew up and hit our heads on the rooftop. Frank tried to reach up for his head. Rodolfo grabbed him tight.

"We have a message. You owe us for coming to our city. We are here to collect. Let us say twenty-five thousand dollars for what you have already done and then fifty percent of anything you get in the future, with maybe a minimum of two thousand a month. We come to collect in two days."

The idea was not to become partners but make it high enough so he could never pay and would run.

"Now get out."

We had not rehearsed this next part. Efraím did not stop. Ricardo tried to throw Frank out, but slipped and fell out on his rear. He was big and bounced. Frank dropped on top of him. Efraím stopped the car and started to back up. I yelled.

"Do not run over them." It was in Spanish but everyone knew there was a gringo accent up front. Efraím turned toward me and did one of his stares. "Maybe he did not hear." I whispered.

Ricardo limped toward the car. Frank limped faster, hobbling the other way towards some bushes and scrub, away from the roadside.

We threw Frank's wallet at him and drove off, tossing up gravel and looking like a cop movie.

"Nice work, Santo. When the rumor starts that an American DEA is here or that a gringo drug lord operates in Oaxaca, we will know how it started."

I pulled off my mask. Everyone was looking at me.

Efraím looked over his shoulder into the back seat, "And good work, my two colleagues. You did well. You will get your cabs and graduate from the bicycles. You have done well."

Efraím was pretty good as a thug. I hoped he had not found his calling. He made a great friend, and thug and friend were not compatible.

Efraím drove us to his house and pulled out four cervezas when we flopped in his front yard chairs. None of us had much experience at this type of thing—that was obvious. The R boys were shaking, Efraím kept laughing too hard, and I was silent.

"Roberto, your crook will leave, I am sure. Do not worry."

I was not worrying. I was trying to figure out if this crime chapter was finished. I hoped it was.

"Cab drivers will keep an eye on him. He will sneak out on a cheap bus, and you and your daughter will be free of him." I figured Randy had been free of him since she shut down his FfA website after I called. It was Efraím and Oaxaca that were now freed of him after this kidnapping business.

But Frank would go someplace else. And do it again. He had to work to live and what could he do? What he knew, petty crime. I was sure. But he would not do it here.

I took off the coat and tie and felt a pleasant tiredness after our night's work. My best Santo Gordo job yet, I thought. The two Rs went to sleep in the corner. Efraím offered to drive me home.

"I have to return this monster SUV soon anyway. The judge might miss it in the morning." Efraím knew more people than just taxi drivers, I now knew for sure. He was moving up.

****

I had never been part of a goon squad before. That was what my mind called the four of us throwing Frank out the car door. I saw him fly. Of course, Ricardo went first and broke Frank's fall. But we four did it. Our Oaxacan vigilante goon squad.

Handing out justice was common out in villages. Maybe in the city, too. You heard about crooks and rapists lynched. We goons did not go nearly that far. And Frank got what he deserved. I was sure. I knew Frank was a jerk, but I kept feeling he was my jerk after our little trip together.

He stayed on my mind all night after Efraím dropped me off.

I thought about him the rest of the week too, but my thoughts grew weaker. Frank got what he deserved, I kept saying.

And what about poor Ricardo? Of course he was doing penance for blowing up the bakery, so some bruises were all right.

Día de Reyes

The week ended with yet another religious bang. Well, more of a whimper, only a few rockets for the Three Kings Day fiesta. This fiesta day was not awaited as eagerly as the others—it was a gentle let down to end it all after Navidad. Except for the children expecting presents from the kings. The Three Kings showed up each year with frankincense and myrrh and all that gold for baby Jesus, but this year they also carried a remote control race car for Domingo and Barbie dolls for the nieces. Yes, Barbie had sneaked in to Oaxaca, along with Sponge Bob and us other border jumpers.

The fiesta began. We sat at tables in the courtyard, singing and celebrating. We downed tamales, we sipped at our chocolates, and we waited for the *rosca*, the special cake, the oval, sweet-dough cake, filled with dried fruits and a handful of pink, bite-sized, rubbery dolls–baby Jesus dolls. There used to be only one Jesus baby in there, and it was lucky to get him in your slice, but now the bakers threw in a half dozen for the big cakes. It was easy to get one.

The rule was if you got one, then you would be a godparent for the next big religious fiesta, *Candelaria*, coming up in February. You would help pay. And you got to buy the big baby Jesus doll a new suit, too. He would be going to church for Candelaria and needed to look flashy. It was lucky to find a Jesus in your slice. Expensive lucky.

I kept thinking that the little Jesus dolls in the cake looked just like the ones that lived in my sister's dollhouse when we were kids. She posed her little pink, rubber doll family in scenes she learned from television and radio. Mommy doll waited for papa doll to come home from work and baby doll slept. The rubber dog waited too. A lot like in the Señora's big *nacimiento*, her nativity scene in the courtyard, where the Virgin Mary mama doll sat watching her baby doll Jesus lying in the manger. Shepherds and animals watched too. José was there. He never went to work. He just hung around.

I always got a baby Jesus in my slice of rosca and had to pay for the upcoming Candelaria fiesta. I was one lucky guy. Jesus found his way into my slice and laughed when I bit him. One year I took off a chunk of his leg, but I kept that quiet.

The Señora handed me my rosca slice. I only had one arm working, the one in the cast was asleep, but one good arm was enough. I probed around with a fork, like a doc, hunting a bullet lodged in some criminal with a hole in him.

I hit something, a false alarm, a dried apricot. The slice looked safe after probing, and I was ready to bite in when Lupe touched my arm.

"Teléfono. Para usted."

Randy called. She had news. I had news too but I planned to keep quiet about Frank's little ride.

"I think you are wrong. Oaxaca Chocolate is not what you think." Randy was in a passionate mood.

"What is it then?" I was in my get-back-to-the-table mood.

"They are a great company. I met with them. They have a team helping to set up cooperatives growing cocoa down there."

"They were behind my bakery explosion. I know it."

"You need to talk with that cab driver friend of yours. He seems like the shady one to me. Is he trying to blame the explosion on the company? They are a good company. I keep telling you."

It went on this way a while. Finally she told me they had fancy holding company name. Oaxaca Chocolate was just a project. That was why I could not find it on the web. They were in a place called Alameda, in the San Francisco area, near her. She gave me an address.

She and I were not seeing eye to eye on this one. "You come into Mexico with a company pushing out little guys and anything can happen." She should know that.

"They are working for the little guys."

Yea, sure. I did not say that out loud. She had been brainwashed. And she was a smart cookie. I was worried.

"You have to remember that investors are coming down to Latin America, no matter what, and this one is starting co-ops and going organic and fair trade. It is a lot better than General Amalgamated Genetic Monster Foods, or some creature like that."

"I want them all to stay away."

"You are part of the problem, running around with your cabbie friends and old fart gringos. You should be doing some good down there or come home."

That should have hurt. But it just made me not want to talk any more. I can sulk with the best of them.

We said goodbye, sounding distant. A chocolate company and maybe a lot more had bulged up between us again.

I sat there a moment letting it sink in. Oaxaca Chocolate or whatever they called themselves was coming. I needed to tell Efraím and go up to San Francisco to do something. With or without Randy's help.

About then my stomach remembered the rosca slice. It was waiting.

Two baby Jesus dolls discovered hiding in cake slices sat in the center of the table. One had icing still on its head. The Señora and her daughter-in-law were going to be the upcoming madrinas.

I bit into my slice feeling safe but, just like every time before, I caught a Jesus between my teeth. He had been hiding behind some raisins. I was careful not to bite off a leg or swallow the guy.

This almost-cannibalism never worried me. Everyone coughed up their Jesus, no one actually ate him, not like with the communion wafers at mass.

Most people did pay for finding Jesus. They gave food money to the Señora for the next party. Some tourists slunk away. But they were never invited back.

I would go shopping soon with the Señora to buy the little guy a new suit and give money for the rest. I paid my Oaxaca dues.

Things slowed down at the fiesta. Families left, taking home the extra tamales. I stayed behind, alone, sitting there, thinking about what Randy had said. What could have happened to her?

I wanted her for some help with Oaxaca Chocolate. No longer.

Who knows, I might start asking Jesus for some help. The three of them sat on the table looking at up me like they might say yes. I smiled at them, but first I would go see Efraím.

****

Efraím came over early Monday after Randy's call. He said he had something for me.

I started talking first. "Oaxaca Chocolate is still in business, setting up cooperatives for growers. It has money. We need to plan."

"I already did." Efraím reached in his coat pocket. "These are for you."

They were plane tickets. I had a day to get ready and then I was flying.

"That was fast." I was not sure if I should thank him for buying the tickets when they were for some work he needed. "I will go. We will figure this out."

"I want you to do more than figure things out, I want you to stop them from coming here."

I had a hard time responding because I had no idea what I would do. They were a big company. I was an old retired expat. I could call reporters, I could post on line, but it did not look like I would have Randy's help to march in front of headquarters.

Efraím patted me on the back, like a coach having to throw in a third stringer at the end of the game. "You are Santo Gordo, remember that."

I went home and packed. It was easy. I left everything comfortable behind and found my suit. I decided not to tell Randy I was coming. I would call her when I got there. She could not argue that way. Well she could, but she could not do anything about it.

****

The airport was chilly in the early morning. I was leaving, but I was not leaving my worries.

My big worry was Oaxaca Chocolate. I was flying up to bargain with them. They were money. They were power. I was only right–the best way to lose any negotiation. I learned that when I was working. Now I was running off like a naive kid, righting wrongs. Like that one stopping tanks in China. Like many people who got steamrolled and flattened.

But travel takes away your thoughts. New sights impinge on your day to day routine. Your mind gets occupied. Travel blocks the throbbing worries that underlie any life. I needed that.

I looked out the waiting room and watched a groundsman on the tarmac pushing a loading ramp and snugging it against the body of a plane. I watched birds feeding around the walkway. I watched the sky waiting for me.

A woman opened the doors, held a battery powered megaphone to her mouth and yelled *"con cuidado."* I was pushed forward, then we bunched at the ramp. Women in heels struggled going up. Some pulled off their foot killers and did the climb in stockings. Flip-flop kids from the States went up carefully. A couple of young guys two-stepped it. Old guys like me stopped half way for a breathing break.

I carried only a small bag–that was it for this trip–but even that weight was too much for a straight shot to the top. Up eight feet, I let the line of people struggle around me.

Efraím had driven me here. "Now go get them. Remember how we handled Frank." I would not take the chocolate company for a ride. This was going to be complicated. Worry had a way of sneaking in.

I took a deep breath, held on to the rail with my good arm and looked down the body of the airplane, trying to get back in my travelling mood.

I was flying one of the new cheapy Mexican airlines that bought a couple of old planes and a lot of fresh paint. I studied the side panels rippling in and out along the window line right up to the nose. This plane had flown far too many trips through bumpy skies and was ready for rest. How many more flights could it have left in it? The paint did a cover-up, but its bright, cheery greens and reds going whoopee every which way could not change the fact that this airplane had done its duty and needed to go out to pasture. Like me. Instead we were both heading north.

I was doing the quick one hour up to Mexico City and then waiting six purgatory ones—can they be anything else in an airport?—until I flew out on another cheapie, a stateside one this time, with a tricky marketing name, but one you could forget easily in case the airline went belly-up.

I climbed the rest of the ramp and saw the plane's interior purples and yellows and reds blossoming in the seats and bulkheads as the crowd behind me filed in, sitting helter-skelter, covering the company artwork with their sweaty flesh and rumpled clothes. The insides might as well have been undecorated—I could only see bodies hanging over the seat edges and poking into isles.

I was guilty of criminal protruding. I am a seat-and-a-half kind of guy even when I am not wearing a cast. Luckily the family beside me was not greedy. They stuck their six year old beside me. He took only a quarter seat and gave me the rest.

The stewardess swung the door shut, read the safety announcements in accented English and mumbly Spanish. Then we took off up over the dry cornfields south of the city.

I was always careful to pick the left side of the plane so I could get a look at the ruins of Monte Albán when we tilted the wing down and made the turn over the hill where the pyramids stood, the place Randy and I had visited a couple of days back. Back when she was the real Randy, not the new converted one.

I could see my tree, the ball court, and the pyramids. They were built to last, just like my old bakery.

We climbed into the clouds and the ground disappeared. It showed up in half an hour as the plane nosed down and the pilot pulled up on the wing breaks. Their thin sheets of metal rose up from the wings into the 400-mile-an-hour windstream, grumbling, shuddering, shaking, and slowing the plane. Some passengers crossed themselves. Some slept through. Most just waited, having heard descents and landings for years, learning which metallic creaks and groans were OK.

I listened. I never trusted tons of airplane hanging in the sky, balanced on a few clouds and some old physics laws. I liked rocks and dirt under me. I got some with a thump and bounce, landing hard and then streaking past the terminal and repair yards, breaking and slowing as we continued towards the dry lake at the end of the runway. The pilot did a nifty quick turn almost touching the grass with one lowered wing, and we crossed over to the long airport taxiway, joining a line of slow rolling jets, moving like a procession of old men. We passed everything, the gates, the terminal, and all the planes, to move into to a no-man's land at the other side of the airport. Finally the wheels stopped with a grab, the engine wound down, and everyone stood, reaching at their overheads, waiting, cell phoning, stretching as a monstrous bus pulled toward the plane and rose on its hydraulic haunches. The stewardess swung open the cabin door, and we docked, like some rocket to a space station, awaiting another go signal. Businessmen and kids who knew this routine twisted through the aisles, getting front row bus seats. We steerage passengers sweated and waited and finally trudged ahead through the hatchway. One guy in the back kept saying, "We all get there at the same time, don't push." Everyone pushed, praying for air conditioning to blow anything but the next guy's smells our way.

The bus, looking like a 747 with snipped off wings and tail, tucked itself down on its wheels and drove us a quarter mile to a naked doorway twenty feet high in the terminal. The bus body rose once more to align itself and we packed out through the exit, excited to be somewhere, acting as though it might lead to something interesting, not just another waiting room.

I walked the half mile through the terminal from the arrival gate to the international lounge. I passed two Starbucks, of course, but mostly I went by Mexican stalls filled with giant sombreros, tequila bottles, and the ceramic tchotchkes, the kind that litter the homes of travelers the world over. I ate my last Mexican meal for a while, too, premade and terrible. Perfect for air travel.

Time passed. I watched. Americans readied themselves to leave with a bottle of water and a book. I prepared myself to be surrounded by Americans and their chatter.

I had gotten to the point in Spanish where I could understand, but still could switch off understanding. If I did not pay attention, words just burbled and mumbled in my head with no meaning. The same as a river or a storm. They made sounds, not words.

English on the other hand, always came in clear and usually loud. I understood everything, even when I wanted to miss it. "Oh my God's" and "actually's" and "whatever's," bombarded my brain space, unwanted and unavoidable. I was trying to desensitize myself to the coming days of 360-degree English by sitting next to a dozen California-bound beach brains. But they put my ears on overload–I needed to wade in gently–so I moved to a Wisconsin group toting canes and pushing walkers, but mostly snoozing.

Time came, I wedged in, the plane took off, and I got to San Francisco. Immigration was a snap after they did a check on the cast. I shook it for them, and it did not rattle. I was afraid they were going to put me in line X, the bad line, but the officer just smiled and pointed me through. TSA must have moved me back on their good-guy list.

I climbed up to the airport subway stop–the BART is what they called it–and then rode underground most of the way, beneath the bay and finally coming up for air in time to see the port on the other side with its white container

213

cranes lining the docks, like a steel-beamed herd grazing on the remains of Oakland. I finished off with a bus ride and climbed down near a coffee shop a mile from the address Randy had given me for the Oaxaca Chocolate project headquarters.

I had travelled ten miles from the airport to a funny city across the bay called Alameda, a good Spanish name, but an all-American town. I found no Zócalo there, only a main street with mostly two-story shopfronts. Mostly local. Maybe all local. A couple of bars. Restaurants aplenty. Hundred-year trees on side streets. A greasy spoon or two. A restoration of my teenage Main Street. A time warp.

They gave it another name, Park Street, as though the city did not know what it had sitting there—a perfect main street. It was my childhood. Maybe the childhood of everyone my age.

I walked by an ice cream shop, an anachronism on any other street, with handmade signs and that smell, the one that surged up in a mixture of remembered teenage dread and adventure wrapped in ice cream, fudge, and candies. Kids in white paper hats holding scoops were loading cones. As I did as a teen.

But the customers were from a different time zone, a zone fifty years ahead of the soda jerks and marble counter.

They were not the teens in my memories. They sported cargo pants, not my madras bermudas. No ring-neck tees like I had worn, only high-tech bicycle shirts and short sleeve plaids. And the girls, no poodle skirts anymore, but an assortment of covers, some drooping in the back, some short in the thighs, some no more than pajamas, some only tights. No big hair survived for them, only red and blue green and sometimes blonde. With tattoos everywhere. Even mothers were tattooed, from shoulder down below their blouse tops, parading babies, almost like they did when I was a teen, but their carriages no longer held the babies I remembered, the ones in white lace suits and bonnets. Babies on Park Street were not dressed, they were decorated, toyed up, clothed like teddy bears or wearing tutus and animal-ear hats. They rode, not in carriages evolved from cribs and pony carts, but in space age, overdesigned ten-wheelers. Some baby cargos were not even human. Fluff dogs in hundred-dollar jackets and tiaras looked out from their screened-in rides. This was the future.

I should have been ready. I had seen them down in Oaxaca–well, at least the human ones, but here these people were everywhere, and on this main street they were attacking my memories.

Forcing me to remember who I had been and worse, who I still was.

This was a main street museum, one that had struggled through dry times while its equals across the US turned into zombie zones sucked dry by freeway big box retailers, which laughed at the 99-cent stores, Salvation Army Thrift Shops and iron-grilled liquor shops they left in their wake. This street made me think about who I was no more and what was no more here in America. And what still was in Oaxaca.

I walked the last few blocks, rolling my suitcase with my good arm and going down Park Street towards the bay. I found my motel, a block from the water. It, too, looked museum grade, clean, functional, but not one to attract attention these days when people want to think they are rich when they travel.

I checked in and looked out my window, hoping to see a '50s beach town with a boardwalk to complement the buildings in my main street memory. Instead, a mall crowded up against the sand. Across its parking lot I could see the far outlines of San Francisco, hazed in the fog. But no taffy shops, no merry-go-rounds, no boardwalk.

Boxy store clones, the same as any in other mall blocked most of my view. They were busy. People were driving up and back, hunting spaces. They came, they parked, they bought. I bet the mall sold more in a day than their main street did in a week. The main street was style, entertainment, diversion; the mall, strictly sales.

The mall had siphoned off some of the city, but not all. The malls mushrooming outside Oaxaca threatened to siphon off everyone local and turn the downtown Zócalo into a tourist Disney-Mex attraction, a zone run by Speedy Gonzales and the Cisco Kid, not Mickey and Donald.

I shut the window and my thoughts. I needed to focus on chocolate. Instead, I lay down and passed out. I was tired. I was getting old.

Sleep lasted an hour. I woke and everything came back to me. I was worn out, I had one bum arm but I was Santo Gordo. I was on a mission.

I called Randy.

"I told you they're a good company. They don't want Oaxaca, they just want to help."

"I need to see for myself. I really do. That was my bakery, the one where I bought my donuts every morning. The one they blew up."

I realized right away that was the wrong way to start out. Donuts were not important to her, people were. Randy was silent on the other side of the phone for a few seconds. Then she started in again, like she was giving me a quick set of one-two body punches to soften me up.

"You have to understand that the people there, the ones in the countryside are incredibly poor, starving poor, deserting-their-villages-and-going-north poor. Someone has to do something. They need capital, they need organizers, they need people who can open markets. That's what I'm working on."

"Why not just let the people living there do that and support them. Why send down your people?"

I was thinking Efraím could run anything. And there were lots of Efraíms in the Oaxaca.

"Look, I'll meet you tomorrow morning. I'll make you an appointment so you can see them. They are not a threat to you. They are doing wonderful things."

****

I slept deep, woke early, and dressed in my suit, leaving the coat hanging over my shoulder with the sleeve flapping, like some fancy Italian movie star. The coat would not fit over my cast. I walked to an espresso joint up their main street. The insides were arty, dark in the back, full of laptops lighting faces too serious for this time of the morning. I took out my phone, my little, embarrassed, screenless guy in this California world of techmania. I called Randy. She would be over soon from her place in the city, the one she still had not invited me to visit.

I ordered a triple. The barista did a performance act, singing customer names and drawing pictures in the foam. No one paid him attention, but I liked the skull he made throbbing in the hot crema. A certificate hanging by the grinder listed him as fourth place in the World Barista Games.

I dunked a croissant, more butter than flour. It melted. Oil rings spread out across the surface as hot coffee currents welled up. The show did not last long. I sipped hard, and soon my brain ticked in. I wanted another but would wait. I did not want to buzz in front of my daughter. Fifteen minutes till Randy arrived, so I took a walk.

The red brick walls of the espresso shop looked Victorian or at least turn of century. You could never build this way in Oaxaca where the earth shook every month or two. Up on top of the walls I counted six ornate brick do-dads, some mason's bad dream, waiting to warn most of us—the ones not crushed—about the earthquake when the shake finally hit in California.

I was antsy that day, nervous. Everything looked off kilter. I had to go see Mister Chocolate. Scare him. But Randy was coming first.

She hopped off a bus and did a limp daddy squeeze. We walked back into the coffee shop.

To start with, she asked about the baby and Lupe. She asked about the Señora. She asked how I was. Not much to tell.

I told her about Frank, her villain–not everything, not what Efraím and I had done to him, only that Frank was leaving Oaxaca. She said he was gone from her website, as though he never existed. She had closed the case.

Then we got down to chocolate business, the hard part.

"You should not have come. This chocolate affair is complicated." She frowned and paused. "I know your friend had his building destroyed."

"Not my friend, the uncle of my friend." I wanted to keep the story straight.

She started over. "Your friend's family lost a building, but I don't think that this company was involved. I received confidential information about their project. I can't tell you everything, but, like I said on the phone, this is a good company. You'll be happy when you hear what they're doing."

"I would be happy if they had not blown up the bakery." She waited for me to finish. She was popping some kind of anger bubble in me, letting it drain. I went on. "And you cannot tell me more? You know something and cannot tell me?"

"I don't know about their issues in Oaxaca."

I hated the word "issues." It was another of those words that happened after I grew up. Value-neutral, existing in a world free of guilt, victimhood, and abuse. I had values, my bakery was the victim, and someone should be guilty.

219

Randy kept going. "I've been discussing operations with them. This chocolate company will be a model, the example we've been waiting for. A big company, very big, with the potential of being Starbucks big, dedicated to the natural, organic, sustainable, responsible, green, fair-traded, direct from the farmer, you name it." She was out of breath but looked like she wanted to go on and on. "They will change the game. The playing field will be moved in our direction."

Where did she learn all this gooped-up talk? I wanted to spank her like when she said her first bad word.

"You need to talk with them, not confront them."

"They blew up my friend's bakery. At least, their money blew up my friend's bakery. I need to hit them with that."

She was quiet for a second. I thought I stopped her, but she recovered with a smile like a mother's to a misbehaving child, "I know money is shit, but shit makes things grow. We want this company to grow well. It is trying to do good."

I wanted someone to do good for Efraím and his uncle. Not the big "good," the G-word excreted by corporate PR.

Randy was not the same. She had been contaminated. I wanted to shake her.

"I want to work with them. I can help them do good. And do it well. I have talked with them. I want them to work with my NGO."

I liked it before when she just helped people a little. I did not blame Randy completely for the good thing. I blamed Google. All the good oozing out of Silicon Valley scared me. Google started it with their "don't be evil" mission. Then things escalated into a PR war, imagine

Mother Teresa brawling with Pope John Paul. "Do Good Well," they said. Corporate saints fought in ads and maybe with their wallets, but only a little with their wallets.

I knew one day, one bad day, when balance sheets tilted down towards hell, all good would be ripped out of their spreadsheets by some newly appointed CEOs. Good is not a part of business. Business is money, and as my daughter said, "money is shit." Everyone knew that. Good and money are from different planets.

"Like I told you earlier, I think you need to do this alone." Randy cold-fished me. She probably had to. She was betting on this chocolate place.

"You don't get the chance often in life to make a big difference. I know my NGO helped, but it wasn't world changing. This company could be. If it succeeds in doing what it plans, then many people will be better."

Not Efraím and his uncle, not me. That was what I was thinking.

"They know me, so last night I made you an appointment with a higher-up. A VP. She'll listen to you. I wouldn't be any help, anyway. You know the story of what happened, I don't. Try to explain it carefully and calmly. Try to work with them. I want to trust you on this."

I was going it alone over at the chocolate company. I had thought I needed help. But she needed them, not me. I needed to scare everyone away from Oaxaca. I was afraid they would never leave it alone.

Oaxaca was in for it, I was sure. It topped the new, hip do-good list. They loved Oaxaca—it had the poor and it had good living too. Perfect for dipping down to give a little help-the-needy time and then coming up for a fancy nightcap drink. Being hip and doing good went together, too, like being old and doing donuts. Oaxaca was lost, I was sure.

"I want you to tell Oaxaca Chocolate about their problems. I think they want to know. But this explosion was an anomaly, I'm sure." She was looking into my eyes better than any hypnotist, not daughtering herself to me anymore, but acting the expert from a new world order. Making me see the big picture. I was stuck on the small one.

"And I have their business name for you, Pretty Good Companies. Oaxaca Chocolate was a code name used inside the company a while back. They do not use that name anymore."

I was on my own. Time to let her go. She had her work to do. I had mine. Pretty Good Companies was in my sights.

We hugged, formally this time. I thanked her for the information, trying not to be sarcastic. She used to bait me for defending the big guy. She led marches for the little ones. Now I was about as little as anyone could get. And she was joining the other side.

I waved a long goodbye at the bus as she rode away.

The head office for Pretty Good Companies was in another part of Alameda, the industrial section. My idea was to go see the VP or whoever it was that Randy had gotten an appointment with and show him a picture of the blown up bakery, the scar on my head, my arm in a cast, and the chunk of cement that I had carried on the plane. Then ask "What gives?" Not a great plan, but a plan.

I went there. I had my pictures in one hand and my concrete in the other. A woman in a suit came out, dressed exactly as some executive in an expertly cast movie would, a real Ms. Business, short straight hair pushed back, a strong stride, reaching toward me, no polish, but a manicure. We shook hands.

"I am here to talk about Oaxaca." I took the lead and sat my concrete and the pictures on her desk. She stared at them, composed herself and looked up.

"Oaxaca, what a wonderful place." No mention of the concrete. "I toured the city when we searched for our flagship store site. I wish we had chosen it." She looked back at the concrete, but she was smiling.

"You are not Oaxaca Chocolate?" I wanted to make sure Randy had the right info. I was worried they had fogged her brain.

"That was one of the names we talked about. We played with the idea quite a while. Don't you love the internal near rhyme. It would have been a winner."

"Well, what are you then? I mean besides that nothing name, Pretty Good Companies."

She squinted at me, like I had said something vulgar, lewd, or at least anti-American. I just wanted information. I did not care whether they changed the name to Chongo Bongo Chocolate, I wanted to know what they were going to do to my home, Oaxaca, the city I had grown to love.

"We are Pretty Good Companies. We are a fine food venture capital company. Now what can I help you with?"

That stopped the I friend you, you friend me talk.

"I have come to discuss your dealings with a property in Oaxaca." I wanted to sound lawyerly. "The Rodrigo Martinez Panadería Building that was blown up by your agent trying to buy it for your business."

"I can tell you that we are not locating in Oaxaca; therefore, we would not be procuring any real estate."

"But you encouraged someone. I want my friends to have justice. Now they have a blown-up bakery."

Ms. Business must have pushed some kind of alarm. I had pushed my anger button. It raised my volume and had me standing waving the concrete chunk. "This is what was left. You blew it up." A large man in a suit walked in. I was expecting a guard.

"Mr. Evans, what is wrong?"

What a caring voice this man had. He must be the company spokes-shrink. I was going to get the treatment.

"I am sure you know about our mission statement. 'Do good profitably.' But it sounds like you think we have a problem."

He was looking at Ms. Business. Mr. Shrink had gotten a signal. They were a great tag team. I was going to get body slammed, I was sure.

"Now can you explain this explosion in Oaxaca issue in detail? Can I see the pictures, the concrete?" He had been listening in. They took my concrete like it was a weapon, not evidence. They were ready for me.

I laid it all out—government harassment, two spikehairs, tattoos, cut hose, explosion, mysterious bulldozer, my head, my arm, Tío Rodrigo. I left out Efraím. It took twenty minutes.

"It sounds like you have had a terrible time."

I never understood how some people could drip compassion. He must have gotten paid a lot. He was good. Ms. Business, however, watched nose-up like some boat plowing through bumpy waters. Then she realized it was her turn and took over.

"I am sure that you understand we cannot be responsible for what other people do. We would like to help you, but we were only in Oaxaca for one day, and we never talked to your friend, Mr. Martinez."

"I do not want anything for me, I want Mr. Martinez to have his bakery. Maybe you could put your chocolate store near him and rebuild the building?"

"As I told you, we are not locating in Oaxaca. We have discussed this with your daughter, and she agreed with us. She asked us to meet with you, and we would like to explain in detail, but we need you to sign a release for that. One that promises you will keep our trade secrets."

They played the good daughter card. I sat down.

She pushed another button and a new face came in the room. This guy was small--he did not smile, swung his bare athletic arms, walked like he was going somewhere in this world, and held a sheet of paper. Mr. Compassion slipped out the door. Mr. Lawyer came in.

"We must ask you to sign a non-disclosure if you want to learn more."

I wanted to hear more, and I figured I could always hide in Mexico if I broke the rules. I nodded. The lawyer came forward. He started a chant, a ritual incantation, explaining how he would personally dismember me if I ever told anyone anything that I was going to find out in the next five minutes. At least it sounded that way from the tone of his voice

"How long is this for?"

"The length of the nondisclosure term is one of the items nondisclosed."

Ms. Business spoke softly "I can tell you it will not be long. Maybe a day or two."

The lawyer pulled out a pen that Freud would have had fun analyzing and handed it to me. I dribbled ink on the page and signed. The lawyer left, repocketing his pen.

There were only two of us. Ms. Business smiled and handed me a pamphlet to read and explained, "Oaxaca Chocolate is no more. It never was. The company name will be Antigua Chocolate. Please read the press release that will be coming out tomorrow."

"You had me sign and go through this and you are going to tell the world tomorrow."

"Yes, this is a delicate time."

I started reading the handout:

> **Antigua Chocolate** (AC), an enterprise of Pretty Good Companies, LLC, will open forty-three chocolate shops throughout the United States in the next six months. The AC chain will sell drinks and Mayan Bars made of chocolate, blended with spices, nuts, and fruits, the better energy alternative providing authentic energy from the cocoa tree. AC is an organic, fair trade company.

Antigua Chocolate's flagship store will be located in the city square, the Zócalo, in Antigua, Guatemala, home of authentic chocolate.

Each AC branch store will deliver a wide selection of exotic foods from the rainforest, many based on chocolate. The decor will be Mayan. A ten-foot video screen will display a direct, continuous feed from the flagship store's front window in Antigua to every AC shop. We call our innovative introduction to the authentic chocolate lands: *the Table on the Zócalo.*

Anyone from our branch stores can sit, sip a chocolate, and start a conversation with a native or a chocolate expert from Antigua, Guatemala.

A contest for visits to our Antigua store will be announced soon. Watch for upcoming announcements.

Come and watch the leisurely life of the chocolate lands, talk with local people, and taste the true food of the gods.

Come to Antigua Chocolate.

I did not need to worry about Oaxaca Chocolate anymore. It had moved to Guatemala. My bakery was safe. We could rebuild in peace.

****

Ms. Business niced me a while longer and led me out. There was nothing more to say. They denied everything, they lawyered me, and my bakery was on its own. But they were not going to invade Oaxaca.

I went back to my main street espresso joint to think. It took a while but I figured it out. I had not screwed up. I had done it. Oaxaca Chocolate was dead. Oaxaca was saved.

I had good news for Efraím. No one in the company wanted anything. They were not bothering with Oaxaca. No money was dangling down. My mission was over. I could go home. Santo Gordo had closed another case, successfully.

There were villains, but, as usual, everyone would get away. The chocolate company went south, the spikehairs went to work, and the local gringo hoping to make a bundle, the guy that ordered the threats leading to the explosion—who knows? It was over. I was happy. No one was dead. Not even me.

I ordered a sandwich to celebrate. I needed to fill up and then nap. The morning had me bushed and I wanted to plan my trip back.

I thumbed through the rest of the Antigua Chocolate pamphlet while I munched. Big cocoa pods were on the cover; Mayan princesses inside. A map of the Zócalo in Antigua, not Oaxaca, was the centerfold. The new AC flagship store would be next to a chocolate museum. A cocoa farm with daily tours was just outside the city. Chocolate tastings were ongoing. Antigua was a chocolate tourist dream town, just the place for Antigua Chocolate's global "Table on the Zócalo," with video hookups for all. I wished Guatemala well.

In Oaxaca, you could get a great table on the Zócalo, but you needed to fly a day to get there. You could find Mezcal tastings. You could even find grasshopper tastings, but not chocolate. Maybe that was why Pretty Good Companies decided against Oaxaca. Round one of globalizing was over. Guatemala one, Oaxaca nothing. Oaxaca won.

I read on. The pamphlet detailed AC's search for the optimal chocolate. The story started out a promising read but turned into a business junket promo with pictures. I recognized Ms. Business. She went here and there, sipping and eating, getting a free ride through Mexico, the Yucatan and Guatemala, holding pottery, weavings, and baskets, standing in old buildings and…

I saw him–Mr. Smoking Gun.

Ms. Business was standing in Oaxaca's Zócalo looking toward a big pink building, my donut shop. She stood next to a gringo, one I knew.

It was Joe, half of the Joe and Mary team, my friends. The ones who had invited me and the baby to dinner.

I read the caption, "Joseph Crompton, local chocolate expert, shows the city of Oaxaca."

I let that sink in. Joe and Mary were big Oaxaca boosters. They were always posting pictures. Joe led tours of local gardens for visitors. He was the unofficial greeter for arriving expats. He could convince anyone he was an expert on anything Oaxacan. He figured out what Ms. Business needed. She needed a location. Joe knew the bakery was not connected to any politicians. He was going to package it for her. It had to be him.

He paid the spikehairs who blew up the bakery.

My case reopened. I could not let anyone find out, especially Efraím. Joe was too big a fish in the expat community for Efraím to take on. He would hurt Joe, sure, maybe fatally, but Efraím would be done in, too. The government would get involved. They were investment friendly. They liked big money coming in. They watched out for their gringos. A lot more than for local taxistas.

Some days you know nothing, some days, too much. I knew enough to get someone killed that day. Way too much.

****

I said goodbye to Randy. She had picked me up and drove me to the airport. She did not share much. Me neither. I guess I was OK with what she was doing. She would get fooled like everyone her age did. Like I got fooled.

We pulled up to the airport, and I do not remember much. I flew back, but it was not a triumphant return. I had gotten a chill up there, one in my brain when I learned about Joe.

Oaxaca was the same. It warmed me a little when I landed in the afternoon sun. Efraím was there and drove me back

I buried the Joe information deep in my brain when we talked. Efraím had taught me to keep quiet. I was the Santo Gordo, after all.

"The Oaxaca Chocolate Company is gone."

"Like poof, it blew up." Efraím made an explosion banging his hands on the wheel.

"No, it moved to Guatemala; so everything is OK." It was OK for us, but who knew about Guatemala? I could only be Santo Gordo in one place. The other was on its own.

"They are buying me a new building?" Efraím did a condemned man's laugh when he talked.

"I mean they are not trying to take your old one anymore." That was the best spin I had. It seemed to work. Efraím patted me on the back.

"I knew you could do it. I knew you could."

Santo Gordo rode once again. But Efraím wanted more.

"Did you find out who was their connection in Oaxaca? Who paid to do it?"

It was time to lie. "Someone they flew in. An American woman. Maybe from Mexico City."

Efraím thought out loud. "I found out the name Oaxaca Chocolate from a taxista friend who heard a woman talking on a phone–they always think we cannot speak English. They do not know we lived in their country for years before we came back. He took this woman to the pastelería a week or two before it blew up. She talked about Oaxaca Chocolate. That is how I knew the name."

I let him go on and on. He never mentioned Joe. That was my secret. I needed to keep that one deep. It was better

Efraím thought the bad gringo was a woman. It made it easier to end the case with no harm done.

Efraím had opened a vein. A vein full of anger at what was happening to his city. "If you have money, so much that you can buy anything, you cannot be good. You must give it away to be good, but that would only make others bad. You should bury it and mix it with donkey shit and grow tomatoes on it. Then you would be good."

Sometimes Ephraim got this way. The real guy inside came out, not as nice as the smiling cab driver who picked up tourists at their hotels. I wanted to move on. I changed the subject.

"When do we start rebuilding your bakery? My donut place?"

****

I phoned Joe, and he invited me over. I wanted to nail the case shut.

I showed up on time. We Americans expect that.

Mary opened the door. She was wearing a local blouse, hand-woven, bright with colors. She was bright herself. Smiling and making me feel like the executioner at a party for the accused. I was over-cheery, smiling too hard. I hoped she would not notice. She wanted me to have dinner. I just wanted to drop the bomb on her husband. But I had to eat. This was Mexico and to refuse was a crime. She had set the table for three. I would be a polite executioner. I would eat as she asked.

The house was normal for an expat. Pretty. She had taken Oaxaca colors and hung them everywhere. Curtains were red and green. Rugs with Zapotec intricacies were red and green too. The papier-mâché parrot was green. The plates were red. Expats tried to make up for their lost pastel lives.

Joe came in. We shook. He had a used car salesman smile. You do not see it much down here. Maybe mine looked the same. We sat and Mary got out the food. I nibbled. I could not stomach this much.

I usually showed my thoughts on my face, or someplace close to it. I wore a mask that meal, like the dancers in the street. It was hard to get the food through it.

You could never tell if street dancers were really as mad as the masks made them look when they jumped and chased the crowd. I was the opposite. I held myself still and looked at the food alongside my napkin. It was beautiful, like the evening, like the house, like everything except Joe and me.

"Those were nice days last week." I tried simple conversation just to get through.

"But it was cold at night. We are lucky we brought our electric blankets."

That was the talk. It went on, weather and traffic, like a bad play. But you don't want to get too familiar before you slam down the ax. It might hurt.

We finally got through the apple pie Mary was so proud of. She took the plates. Joe and I went up the metal stairway, spiraling to the rooftop terrace for some man talk. He carried a bottle of something red and Chilean. He poured. I sipped. He drank.

"So why do you want to talk." Joe changed from used car man to hawk. He leaned close to me.

I took a second and looked around. The terrace was perfect like the downstairs. Yellow and blue this time. Glasses, pitcher, lanterns, paper hangings. Rattan chairs. Umbrellas. Planters everywhere, hidden in blooms. Tiny lights strung across the terrace. Up three stories, on the flat roof, it looked out at the postcard church across the alleyway, with its doors opened for evening mass and one or two children playing on the stone-paved church grounds. Purple blooming jacarandas lined the street in front of their home finishing off the scene.

"Why, Joe? Why did you do it? Why the bakery?"

He knew that I knew and played it straight.

"Money. Why do people do anything? For the money. But I never said blow it up. Remember that. I said scare him a little."

Joe was tight, his fists were tight, his lips too, but his words were somehow gentle out of that face. I needed to get things straight from my side right away. "I'm not here to hurt you. I only want to make sure Efraím never finds out. You need to help me on that. I want this mess over."

Joe was silent.

"I don't want you on my conscience, Joe. I believe you. It was business, not crime." I did not believe that, but it relaxed Joe. He leaned back thinking and then decided to spill it. Like something popped inside.

"I knew the Rathman's from way back. They asked me for help finding a place on the Zócalo for their chocolate shop. They sent a woman down to check it out. You need to know someone down here, or you just bleed money in funny fees and obstructions. You bleed even if you know someone, but it helps. They knew me."

He smiled as he looked back inside his head remembering. The chocolate shop was the deal to make him big in Oaxaca. Anything on the Zócalo was important. And he would have been, too.

"The old bakery was ideal. Right location, not tied into anyone in government that I knew about. It would have been good for Oaxaca--jobs, more tourists, chocolate with Oaxaca's name all over the world. I keep thinking of Oaxaca Chocolate in Hong Kong and London and Paris. It would have made Oaxaca."

It would have made Oaxaca more of a mess. Joe was back in used car mode. He went on about the stuff I already knew, more about the Rathman's, about Pretty Good Companies, about the plans for the new chocolate empire. An empire that had its showroom in Oaxaca but its brains and money up north. And reached out everywhere with chocolate shops that hung Zapotec rugs on the walls. Oaxaca Chocolate on every corner. Oaxaca everywhere.

"I was going to buy the bakery for a good price. I hired a lawyer to come here from Mexico City and make good offers. I wasn't going to steal it like some crook. I wanted to be fair."

I did not argue back. He had told me too much, like he wanted me as a witness, or an accomplice, if things went wrong with Efraím.

"You need to leave for a while, let things calm down." I wanted Joe gone forever, but a while was a start. "There could be a leak and Efraím would find out. He is not a forgiving type. If you wait, the bakery will be rebuilt, and everyone will forget everything. Take a vacation with Mary. Maybe the beach, or Guatemala and try some chocolate, or Costa Rica."

Joe looked like that thinking statue. He had his hand on his chin, leaning forward. He was off somewhere in his head. I was hoping he was on his vacation.

"You're probably right."

Mary called up from the apartment, "Would you like to come down for coffee now?"

"In a few minutes." Joe answered and then resumed the vacation thought. "You know I like life here, but a break would work out."

A voice on the street started singing accompanied by a near-tuned guitar. We both looked over towards the church but could not see the singer. He was too close to the house.

"He comes every night and plays. His voice is rough, but it is authentic Oaxaca" Joe walked toward the side of the terrace and looked down.

"I drop him pesos. This is one of the reasons I'm here. To hear this. It is the real city. It's my city now."

After the song Joe let go of a bill, twenty pesos, I think. It fluttered down beneath my view. I heard a *gracias* below.

236

I started to walk toward the steps to go down and help Mary. Joe called to me, "Look at this."

He was so natural, so sincere, so hopeful, so happy, I went over. And looked. No one was there. The churchyard was empty. The congregation had started singing inside the church. It was a picture of peace. I relaxed.

Joe patted me on the back like an old friend, and then he pushed. At first a gentle push.

"Sorry, Roberto, you would tell your cab friend. You tell him too much. And he will never forget. You know that."

He pushed harder. He had me leaning over the edge, looking down. Seeing cement and rocks below. I twisted back. He was smiling at me. "Goodbye, Santo Gordo."

I was off balance but swung my cast at him. It hit Joe's shoulder solid and knocked him sideways, not far, just a step. He moved forward to recover and pushed me again, this time with his other arm. He was on the edge with me, palm open, flat on against my shoulder, pushing steady.

My body leaned out beyond the roof edge. Most of my weight was out in space. Only my feet were still on the terrace rooftop. I put my weight on one foot and turned to get away from him, but moved out more into space.

Concrete cracked under my feet. The edges of the flat concrete roofs were always the first to go. They all were black, mold-covered and rotten. I do not know how cement can rot, but it did and sometimes bricks fell with it. Sometimes people, too.

Concrete was cracking, dropping. I was falling. Joe bent awkwardly forward like me. The concrete under him was falling, too. Falling in chunks. He was almost clear of the roof. Then turning back, like a kid on roller skates trying to regain his balance as he went down. Going slowly forward. Arms windmilling. Off to my side. Reaching for me to save him, I think. Touching me with his hand one last time, but not grabbing anything. Pushing me a bit farther away. Coming up hands empty, clutching air.

I had just enough spring in my leg still touching something to push me out a couple feet from the roof. Not far, just a little. Toward a jacaranda, one of the purple blooming trees along the alley. It was not big and about five feet down and springy enough to catch me like a cradle. A hard cradle. A cradle that jabbed and poked. But not concrete.

That last push from Joe saved me. Along with my jump. They put me in the tree, about half way down. Surrounded with purple blossoms, all around my head.

Joe went down head first. Screaming.

Mary screamed, too, a minute later. She had come up on the terrace and was looking down at Joe.

I hung in the tree. This time my chest caught it, not my head. It hurt. My good arm was bent back under me. It hurt. A broken tree branch stuck a little into my chest. Not far. It hurt. I was trapped.

Someone came out and yelled from the church. Mary stood at the edge and screamed more. I made noise, then went quiet. It hurt to yell.

They took me down. An ambulance carried me away, sirens going, lights flashing, the stretcher and me bouncing when we hit the holes in the street. I passed out.

I was finished in Oaxaca. I knew it in the tree. Oaxaca had looked the other way when I had problems before. This time an American died. Investigations would come. Efraím would find out about Joe paying to blow up the bakery and, worse, me knowing and not telling him. The expats would guess something fishy happened. The Señora would know God was not happy.

I was finished. Oaxaca was over. Santo Gordo was done.

About the Author

Charles Kerns writes mystery novels about Oaxaca and California. He first visited Oaxaca thirty-five years ago and now is quite at home on its streets and in its restaurants.

He wrote the first Santo Gordo book in 2012.

He lives near Oakland, California, when not in Oaxaca. While in Oakland, he works a bit at Stanford University Libraries, rides his bicycle on flat tidelands and keeps up on his reading. In Oaxaca he follows in the path of Santo Gordo and enjoys his friends, food and long walks.

**